VanWest
The Past

Book 1 of VanWest Series

Kenneth Thomas

Copyright © 2020 by Kenneth Thomas

All rights reserved. No part of this book may be reproduced or used in any manner without written permission of the copyright owner except for the use of quotations in a book review. For more information, address:

ken@vanwestbooks.com

FIRST EDITION

Written in British English

www.vanwestbooks.com

ISBN: 978-1-8380561-5-5

KDP ISBN: 979-8-6471020-8-9

Cover design by Elementi Studio

Contents

Prologue 1

Chapter 1   The Universal Games 6

Chapter 2   Pytheas's Labyrinth 15

Chapter 3   Forewarned 26

Chapter 4   The Doctor Knows 35

Chapter 5   Time Travel Training 48

Chapter 6   Leap to the City of Light 58

Chapter 7   The Orchestra 67

Chapter 8   Beware the Seductress 75

Chapter 9   Leap into the Queen's Nest 84

Chapter 10 A Forgotten Friend 95

Chapter 11 A Traitor and a Hero 101

Chapter 12 To Serve the Universal 113

Chapter 13 Back to the Cockroach Farm 124

Chapter 14 Leap to Utopia 132

Chapter 15 A Killer's Love 143

Chapter 16 The Past 151

Chapter 17 The Failed Launch 158

Chapter 18 Leap to Judgment Day 166

Chapter 19 A New Beginning 177

Read More 189

Prologue

The exponential growth of long-distance space travel at the beginning of the 22nd century caused Earth's health to decline and its population to plummet. Radiation from spacecraft poisoned crops and caused many people to die, eventually leading to the collapse of Earth's superpowers US and China. By the 25th century, all of Earth's inhabitants were forced to either live deep underground or seek refuge in the cooler and less polluted Antarctic continent. Whilst most suffered terribly a few found it to work to their advantage.

Oligarchs controlled large swathes of Antarctica. Acting as feudal overlords, they enslaved these refugees and forced them to undertake dangerous jobs to earn their keep, such as extracting rare-earth metals in hastily built toxic mines. Those convicted of even the pettiest crimes received a fate worse than the mines; a near-certain one-way trip to their deaths in lunar and asteroid work camps to gather the resources needed for the building of ever-larger space fleets and operations.

Replacing the void left by the fallen superpowers the Oligarchs formed an autocratic governance, later becoming the Universal Council. The addition of high-ranking military officials and influential scientists to their inner circle extended their control and power. Their members began to refer to themselves as the 'Elites'; virtually immortal thanks to major advances in stem cell technology, many are now hundreds of years old. Their fates, in the year 3000, a stark contrast to those of the downtrodden refugees, which they call the 'citizens'.

The Universal Council maintains their power not only through their highly advanced and well-trained forces of Space Army, Inspectors and Enforcers but also through the use of mass propaganda, surveillance, robots, forced famines and purges. Despite all this, opposition survives and, in some settlements, even thrives. The leading rebel group is the Natural Earth Alliance (NEA) who regularly launches skirmishes against the Council.

Many are adherents to a new age religion called Utopianism: its teachings derived from a once-obscure 20th-century philosopher Hans Ashtar. His followers believe that he correctly foretold that any dream of a Utopian world would end by the 21st century due to the rapid advancement of technology and the immorality of machines, which changed human behaviour for the worse. These adherents see it as their mission to restore Earth to its late 20th-century self.

The Universal Council reacts to the rise of Utopianism with an iron fist, using their forces to eradicate the adherents from their settlements. Employing their crack police unit of Enforcers as well as the Inspectors charged with interrogations and obtaining confessions to seek them out. Trained at the Universal's academy located on Earth's moon, and enhanced with bionics, these still mostly human Enforcers are skilled fighters and astute detectives. Even after graduation, they continue to train regularly with the best, and those ranked Captain or Major earn the chance to compete in the annual Universal Red and Blue Games.

The Games serve as an important propaganda tool for the Universal Council to show off the might of its forces by pitting one hundred Blue team Enforcers against one hundred Red team Space Soldiers in a race to the finish.

The Space Soldiers are the most fearsome of the Universal forces, more machine than man, they are cyborgs. Though faster and stronger than Enforcers, their lack of human skills makes them ill-suited for deployment in Antarctica's densely populated settlements. Less apt at differentiating Utopians from ordinary citizens, they risk far too high casualty rates. The Space Soldiers as their name suggests patrol space, monitor asteroid and lunar work camps in the solar system, and more recently, smaller trading colonies alongside the Inspectors. Their use has increased considerably in recent decades, causing some alarm amongst higher-ranked and older Enforcers.

The Universal Red and Blue Games hold a great prize for its one victor beyond just prestige for their team: a fast-track to attaining the rank of Lt. Colonel and becoming an Elite as well as gaining much sought after privileges and opportunities like becoming an Elite guard to one of the Universal Council's immortal leaders.

Each of the last four years has seen a Red team's Space Soldier win, and after each victory, they returned even stronger and more cunning. Their streak is unlikely to be broken anytime soon. Nevertheless, Captain VanWest, a recently promoted Enforcer, will be one of the contestants hoping to break it. Relatively young, he has earned his shot after only two deployments, the last being in the Antarctic settlement of ColaBeers. A lucrative, once troubled, area controlled by the powerful Oligarch, and its Mayor Bramsovica since the 23rd century. It was at risk of being overrun by rebels that is untill VanWest outfoxed its NEA leader.

VanWest was able to foresee her well-planned ambush, beyond simply a gut feeling: He could actually see his enemy laying her trap, leading him to call up extra patrol androids, who encircled the area and helped to capture her. Unlike her fellow rebels, she was not killed immediately. Instead, she was painfully tortured to reveal hidden locations before being executed in front of the citizens on 'Judgment Day'.

VanWest keeps his ability a secret from the Universal Council, never having felt quite at ease with who he is or with his masters. During his tours he has seen and done many a questionable deed in their name - all of, which were justified under the Universal

Council's commandments and the Enforcer motto of 'the progression of man and the Universal'.

His promotion to the rank of Captain gave him the chance to compete for this Elite prize under the tutelage of the Blue team's last winner Colonel Cornelius, referred to simply as the Colonel. Strict and demanding, the Colonel has rigorously trained VanWest and his ninety-nine fellow Enforcers for every scenario that could possibly occur during the course.

A man of few words, his mere presence intimidates. His hair short and white, his shoulders broad on a muscular frame, he glowers at all who dare to look him in the eye. Beyond being strong and tough, his edge is an unrivalled ability to adapt his tactics to changing situations and threats as he demonstrated when he won. Upon winning, the Colonel elected to become the guardian of the SCC-400, a super high-tech weaponised ship used to transport the highest-ranking leaders of the Universal Council.

For his team to have a chance of winning, the Colonel has devised what he believes to be a game-winning strategy. Grouping his Enforcers into twenty-five specialist teams made up of four-man squads with complementary abilities and training each on how to approach a multitude of likely obstacles, which he hopes will increase the chance of at least one Enforcer being victorious at long last.

This year the Universal Games are being held inside a magnetic dome on the mountains of Crete, the former Greek island situated in the incarnadine brine of what was once the Mediterranean Sea but is now a barren landscape with extremely high levels of radiation. The event is broadcasted to all the citizens of the Solar System; and although no theme has ever been exactly alike, each stage will be progressively more difficult and dangerous than the previous.

Carefully choreographed, no competitor is shown to look scared or weak. With team communications kept from the citizens, the Universal Council wants to project an imperious facade showing how their Enforcers and Soldiers are able to overcome obstacles that no mere human can to build respect, win admiration, and intimidate any would-be enemy.

Those on Earth tune in virtually with their 4D hologram form filling the stands. Awarded a rare day off to celebrate and pay tribute. This year's theme, decided by a commission made up of Elites, is that of a neoclassical Romanesque and Greek course comprised of three arduous stages, divided by walls of green and orange light.

Only the names of the stages, inspired by the Antiquities, have been released beforehand, giving a small clue on what to expect:

>Stage 1: Sprint through Jupiter   (to Green)
>Stage 2: Pytheas's Labyrinth   (to Orange)
>Stage 3: Fires of Vesta   (to White)

With the exact details to be unveiled as the race progresses, it promises to be full of shock and gore for competitors and citizens alike.

Chapter 1   The Universal Games

The citizens' 4D holograms light up the arena as they tune in for the most anticipated event of the year. An event like no other, the annual showpiece of the Universal Council is an action-filled course built to test its finest Space Soldiers and Enforcers. The prize for its one winner is the ultimate dream of many a man, woman and child watching today: the status of 'Elite' along with all its trappings.

Their claps echo across the magnetic dome as the Blue Enforcer team enters. Captain VanWest is amongst those marching towards the team's neon blue-lit starting grid. Slowing only to salute the team's base commander Colonel Cornelius. Seated high above in the command tower readying to guide them to their first win in five long years.

Upon reaching the team's neon blue grid, the Enforcers crouch down, assuming a sprint take-off position with their hands placed in front and their left leg bent slightly further back than their right. Awaiting the arrival of their most formidable opponents the Red team's Space Soldiers, the citizens continue to clap expectantly, albeit at a slower and more rhythmic pace than before.

Beside VanWest are the other members of his four-man squad: to his right is his academy classmate Barys and left are Alpha and Kun-lee. Like him, they were all recently promoted to the rank of Captain after their last tour of ColaBeers as thanks for their successful expulsion of the NEA rebels from the mining settlement. All are rookies; thus they are ranked outsiders with only Alpha receiving decent odds of winning at 50-1 due to his distinction of holding the academy's record in the 1-mile sprint - a distinction that perhaps earned him the designation of being their squad leader and, more pertinently, the right to finish first in the unlikely event that they all make it to the end of Stage 3. By comparison, VanWest's odds, as calculated by the Elites of the Games Commission, are dismally low, 150-1. Past performance is said to be the biggest factor; and with these odds, he will exceed all expectations by completing Stage 1.

All Enforcers are trained since youth under a system inspired by the stories of ancient Greece and the Spartan boys, which emphasises discipline, endurance and, above all else, duty, teaching all to follow a strict code of honour to one another. The Enforcers must never show fear and appear stolid no matter what. Whilst VanWest's face does well to hide his anxiety, he has rarely felt so nervous. His heart beating faster and louder with every moment that passes, and his body cringing with every clap. He manages to retain his composure by staring straight-ahead and slightly down, away from those watching in the stands.

Though VanWest aspires to gain Elite status one day and finish well, he's neither cocky nor stupid. He appreciates the honour of just being a competitor. Even though he is in superb condition and fitness, he only does well to match that of his fellow Enforcers. His height of six-foot-two inches is average, well below that of the Space Soldiers due to emerge soon. Looking across, each contestant packs powerful frames and bulging biceps into their tightly fitted blue body armour, everyone looks formidable!

Unlike the Space Soldiers, the Enforcers are an eclectic bunch. Barys, a straight-talking stocky chap, has distinctive purple eyes, and Kun-lee, with a perfectly tuned athletic body, has bright red hair. What unites the Enforcers is not their appearance but rather their fervent dedication to serve their masters, the Universal Council. Boldly written across their chest plates is their motto *Pro Progressio Hominis et Universales*, for the progression of man and the Universal, a derivation of the second Universal Council commandment. A commandment that has been used to justify many a morally questionable act.

The Enforcers' battle uniforms are identical except for their helmets. Each has been custom designed to feature an approved brand from one of its Elites. VanWest's features the food brand logo *InsectnOut*, Earth's largest food distributor, renowned for their freshly made and succulent cockroach burgers. The company is owned by a business family of Elites called the Huberts. Their gift of this most superior and lightweight of helmets is in part thanks to him having saved the head of their family from a deadly bombing during his first tour.

Each member of VanWest's squad has elected to equip themselves with the same three items on the Colonel's recommendation: an energy shield, a laser sword, and rifle over a jetpack and sling belt of grenades. Though in Stage 1 these items will not be active, they could be tremendously useful in Stage 2, *Pytheas's Labyrinth*.

The rising sound of heavy footsteps signals the Red team's arrival. Their steps accompanied by a chillingly monotonous and repetitive military chant of 'Universal' as they proceed past their command tower, saluting their base commander and last year's winner Lt. Colonel Omega, to take position at the team's neon red starting grid. The Space Soldiers are noticeably taller and stronger looking, their biceps bigger and shoulders broader.

The Soldiers' body armour holds a different Universal commandment than the Enforcers: *Nibus Perdere Universalis Synodus Omnium*; a fearsome warning that translates as 'to destroy all those who defy the Universal'. By appearance, it definitely looks like they are programmed to do so, their faces metallic and heads bald, expressionless and hollow, with beady eyes that stare forward menacingly red - none look quite human each weirdly alike.

Being cyborgs, none have a helmet or a mask as they are able to withstand the contaminated and putrid air still prevalent even inside this dome, this the air of equatorial Earth in the year 3000. Only a few things tell them apart: their unique collection of scars, which they proudly bear on their faces, and the symbols engraved on their shoulder armour. Other than that, only their base commander, Lt. Colonel Omega stands out, sporting thicker and brighter red shoulder pads than the rest.

The loud booming voice of the Games announcer cuts through, 'Citizens! Welcome to the Universal Games 3000! Join me in hailing our leaders, the Universal Council. All Salve the Universal, all Salve thee'. Prompting the citizens to start a succession of loud and slow claps, chanting 'Universal, Universal, all Salve thee'! Eager to see what is about to be unveiled.

Gasp! A bright light illuminates the Games' first stage, *Sprint to Jupiter.* Lying in front of the competitors is a mile-long sprint through a swamp towards a gigantic twenty-foot tall bronze statue of Jupiter, the Roman King of the Gods. It stands imperiously before a temperamental volcano that shoots up large plumes of ash, darkening the skies above the magnetic dome.

This is one mean looking stage! Clearly intended to separate the fast from the slow. As VanWest surveys the course, his earlier nervousness turns to that of fight and survive. He lifts his right knee up and poises his feet, ready to jolt forward, in expectation of the countdown. And, touches his amber stone pendant tied around his neck for a second for good luck. An item he has done well to keep safe, for it's frowned upon for Enforcers to have personal items such as this.

A low screak rings through his ears, his Moggle X lenses activating, with instructions on this course and a message from the Colonel. The message scrolls across, *00:10:00 To Complete* to avoid disqualification, confirming this short stage is focused on speed. As the instruction finishes scrolling the ceremonial horn sounds, signalling for the countdown to commence. VanWest edges his foot onto the gridline as *5* projects high above, its bright green colour contrasting against the black smoke billowing out from the Volcano.

A new clap starts, in sync with the countdown, '*5*', '...*4*', each reverberating in his head, '...*3*', VanWest heartbeat fastens, '*2, 1*'.

'Run Enforcers! RUN'!

Colonel Cornelius yells through the Blue teams' communicators as the countdown hits zero, propelling VanWest forward into the shallow and muddy swamp in front. An obstacle that the Colonel has trained the Enforcers well for.

VanWest finds himself momentarily paralysed, not so much by the sticky mud and freezing water as the whole bewildering spectacle around him. Barys pulls his arm, gesturing him to follow his lead. Together shifting their plasma rifle's butt from side to side, as if an oar of a canoe, VanWest regains his speed and composure. As he progresses through, a new obstacle appears, the ground gives way to sinkholes, forcing him into a series of leaps to avoid the same fate of several other competitors being sucked down. Unscathed, and a little out of breath, he reaches the rest of his squad, which, to his relief, have all made it thus far.

'You are one slow piece of roach goo, VanWest'! Alpha derides him.

VanWest chooses to ignore him, his mind transfixed by the gigantic and eerie statue of Jupiter. Now closer, he sees the volcano's steep and jagged rock face that they must climb to reach the next stage. The statue's bronze hand points forebodingly at them its index finger stretched out as if warning them to go back.

Alpha is unintimidated, he smirks, 'This will be roaching easy'! Thinking that this climb will be the end, with the gateway to Stage 2 at its top. If that's true, then this would have been one of the easiest Games' courses ever - a telling indication of Alpha's inexperience and foolish arrogance. VanWest shakes his head but decides it's better to say nothing. He knows there is more.

As they near the summit, pulling themselves over the rock face with their gear in tow, Alpha is made to eat his words. There's another obstacle before the green light: a rusty wrought iron bridge, partially obscured by black smog, hanging precariously over a stream of molten lava. It twists violently - *screech* - with every new spew of lava shooting up from beneath. As VanWest suspected, a rookie mistake to think that this stage would be anything close to easy.

Indeed, any notion of this is further eroded as they watch a Red Space soldier stumbling across the bridge, completing a slow dance with death. VanWest exchanges a tense look with Barys, who does his best to reassure him, 'Y'all know this was not going to be a moon stroll, but you know we defeated bigger piles of roach goo'!

VanWest is happy to have his long-time colleague Barys by his side. They have been close all through their academy days and tours. One might even call them friends, having stuck together all this time, but 'friends' isn't a used word or even a concept in the Year 3000, at least not amongst Enforcers. All are taught in this Sparta inspired system, to treat each Enforcer equally, to devote themselves to the Universal Council and defer preference only to its Elites.

The Space Soldier's death of dance finally comes to an end as he makes one stumble too many and is caught by the next spew of lava. *Agh!* Screaming from the excruciating pain as it encases his armour and cooks him alive.

Alpha laughs at the gruesome spectacle, 'Space Roach! Good riddance', slapping Kun-lee hard on the back. Kun-lee is visibly unimpressed by Alpha's reaction and gives him a cold stare. Alpha has always behaved like a mindless brute, albeit an Enforcer, his behaviour has never been Spartan as far as VanWest and the others have observed. Nevertheless, he has never been reprimanded.

'Laugh it up'! Barys replies 'You got a plan to stop us getting deep-fried? Do you'?

'Maybe we should just run through it', a nervous sounding Kun-lee suggests, to which Alpha nods enthusiastically in agreement, always keen on anything that involves sprinting.

Barys shakes his head, 'Come on, it is not going to be that simple'!

Their time is ticking down. A reminder from the Colonel rolls across their Moggle X lenses, *00:03:00 Remaining* until disqualification.

VanWest studies the bridge, quickly figuring out how they can complete this challenge. 'Kun, you are partly right, do you see the pattern of the spews? Look at the lava! It splashes over the rails in rhythm. We could all sprint across, one after another'.

'Really'? Kun-lee replies.

'We will need to time it right'! VanWest answers.

Alpha grins, 'I see you are not a total waste of space after all! I'm first up, roachtards'!

Pushing past VanWest and Barys, he hurries to the bridge and, without hesitation, times his run perfectly and sprints across, clearing it in a matter of seconds. The bridge screeches loudly as he finishes.

Kun-lee and Barys follow in sync, racing through the lava spews, dodging each one flawlessly. By the time it's VanWest's turn, the spews of lava have not only changed rhythm but have also hastened, with the bridge screeching louder and louder as it twists. VanWest races forward onto the swinging bridge, doing well to make it to the halfway point before falling to his knees.

He lifts himself up but, worryingly, must now wait for another spew to cross the end of the bridge. As it passes, he hurries forward only for it to twist violently once again, throwing him onto his back. Glancing back, to his dismay, he finds that two blue Enforcers from a different squad have stepped onto the bridge, desperate to finish the race in the allotted time. They appear unaware of the lava spews' pattern and are not waiting for VanWest to finish crossing.

A concerned Barys frantically waves his arms at the other Enforcers, yelling at them to get off, 'Hey-hey, it's too heavy'! But his pleas fall upon deaf ears.

The weight of the Enforcers causes the railing to twist further, screeching dissonantly as it starts to untwine. VanWest manages to crawl towards Barys's outstretched hand, who is just about able to pull him to safety. The chains snap behind him, taking the rusty iron bridge down into the ravine below along with the Enforcers. They cry out in agony as they melt into the lava stream.

'Close call, roachtard! A deadweight! Can't even cross a bridge! Don't roaching cost me my trophy'! Alpha scolds, throwing numerous insults at him. With only 30 seconds to spare, an ego wounded VanWest follows into the wall of green light and enters Stage 2.

Excited citizens cheer them upon their arrival, especially thrilled by VanWest's death-defying bridge crossing. The cheers give him a timely and much-needed boost of confidence, he has also made it further than expected, further than his given odds of 150-1.

'Born entertainer'! Barys jokes, patting VanWest on his back.

At the top of the dome, the Games leaderboard shines red, revealing a heavy toll with only *144 out of the 200* competitors remaining. The red colour is not a warning, rather an indication that the Red team is in the lead. The leaderboard then begins to show the updated odds for each competitor left in the race with the Elites having placed new bets between themselves. VanWest is somewhat pleased to see that his odds have slightly increased to *130-1*, but his squad still trails far behind most. And so too does any realistic chance of winning. Nevertheless, for VanWest at least, there is still honour to be won.

He doesn't have much time to catch his breath as his Moggle X sends through new instructions, this time from the Games commission, on the details of Stage 2, Pytheas's Labyrinth. The first instruction ominously informs him that his *Moggle X Mapping and Orientation Programs Are Suspended*. The second that there are only 2 hours to navigate through a *10-mile* long maze *02:00:00 To Complete*.

'What the flying R!' a flustered Kun-lee grumbles.

'Clean your sticks boys! We are going to need them working'! Barys instructs as he cleans the swamp's mud from his own plasma rifle, the weapons having become active.

'No map but weapons... great'! Kun-lee remarks sarcastically.

'Scared? Stop acting like an injured and crying child'! Alpha tilts back his head and grins. A sick reference, they know to be that of the dreadful massacres during their tour of ColaBeers.

'Screw you! You ugly roach'! A now visibly rattled Kun-lee replies angrily.

Stage 2 is specifically designed by the Games Commission to thin the field in the most entertaining way possible, with the result being that only the strongest and very best competitors make it to Stage 3. Last year's second stage was one of the most perilous, forcing competitors to row over rivers of molten rock whilst fire rained down - the one before that involved battling past giant monstrous and mythical creatures. Both these challenges left 50 competitors active and able to compete for the prize.

Although a maze type challenge is relatively uncommon, it nevertheless holds the grim record of having the highest number of casualties. Mainly as of those who are lost and injured, few are ever rescued or retrieved because Space Soldiers and Enforcers are the only ones able, and trained, to navigate this maze and its dangers. Thus, teammates and superb teamwork are of the upmost importance.

Long 'ohs' and 'ahs' rise as the stage commences with an archway appearing out of the darkness. The arch is decorated with intricate carvings: on the right, a giant bull with large horns, on the left is the face of a man without a nose. Above it, an ancient Greek inscription shines in gold, *Πυθέας ὁ Μασσαλιώτης*, Pytheas of Massalia.

Chapter 2   Pytheas's Labyrinth

Colonel Cornelius, their base commander, radios through, 'Listen up, there are nine possible dangers within the maze... remember no Moggle X available'! And sends through the following list:

Number 1. Murderous criminals armed with lasers
Number 2. Booby-traps, fake floors and trip mines
Number 3. Freezing ice chambers below minus 20C
Number 4. Falling rocks and spikes
Number 5. Thermal weapons, burning oil
Number 6. Sensory turrets set to kill
Number 7. Packs of mutant dogs
Number 8. Gigantic carnivorous insects
Number 9. Sensory deprivation gases causing hallucinations

'Confirm list received, Enforcers! Affirmative'?
'Yes, Colonel. Affirmative'! All Enforcers reply simultaneously. The list isn't a surprise, the Colonel had warned and trained them well for this.

With the communication ended, Barys tries to lighten the mood with a joke, 'They all run out of ideas or what'!

'Seems so', Kun-lee agrees in a serious but slightly quivering, voice, doing his best to keep his nerve and appear stolid.

Barys does his best to motivate, 'Come let's go, we have a game to win'!

'Moon fairies go first though'! Alpha coldly shoves Kun-lee towards the archway.

As he steps forward, the archway opens, releasing with it a deathly low shrill. Reverberating along the walls, the squad instinctively assume a guarded melee formation as they activate their energy shields. VanWest and Kun-lee place their rifles to the front while Barys and Alpha guard the back, opting for their ancillary laser swords to form a defensive square. They proceed cautiously walking as the light from their rifles ominously reveals walls decorated with skulls and bones, like that of ancient catacombs. They have no choice but to proceed. Adrenaline pumps through their veins; it's fight, fleeing is not an option.

They walk until they reach three passageways, each indistinguishable from the other, 'Can't go wrong with the middle, hey'? Says Barys always able to crack a joke.

'After you then... I order you'! Alpha commands, not wanting to put himself at risk. 'Your job is to help me win. No-one else has a roaching chance, got it'?

No one answers, VanWest, Barys and a nervy Kun-lee exchange a nod to each other, cold air whistling past them as they enter. Each step seems to push them tighter together as if the walls are narrowing, each feeling quite claustrophobic and on edge. What on the Colonel's list will they encounter first? The passageway winds nearly endlessly; whichever route they take, it returns them again and again to the same place.

After what feels to be hours rather than a few minutes, they worry if this maze even has an end. Its quietness and lack of dangers thus far most strange, as if it had been set up this way to build suspense. Focussed, the squad does not notice the Games' viewing portals spaced every dozen meters or so, camouflaged as round black blobs. This all a glorified killing spectacle, Universal Council propaganda used to entertain and, at the same time, show off the strength of their forces and their might; inducing fear into any would-be dissenter.

'Good choice, roachtard'! An increasingly agitated Alpha insults Barys.

'Shout your mouth boy! Or I'll stick this laser sword where sun don't shine', Barys replies angrily.

With tensions reaching boiling point, a glimmer of light calls their attention. They hurry forward with a renewed sense of urgency, the light growing brighter. It brings them to a new junction that connects two passageways they haven't come across before.

'This is new', VanWest whispers, too worried to speak louder.

A light above the junction reveals what must be a star and other strange symbols carved into the floor, including what appears to be a boat. As if to give them a confirmation of their progress, their Moggle Xs reactivate and moments later a scrambled transmission comes through.

It sounds like their base commander, Colonel Cornelius, his voice fragmented and distorted, 'Good progress. The path... Pytheas navigator guided... above... using Polaris, affirm... mat... out'.

Barys tries to respond, only to find his Moggle deactivated once again. It shares the same name of the stage and that above the archway, *Pytheas of Massalia*. It must be a clue how to escape *Pytheas's Labyrinth*: a map of sorts to show the way out.

VanWest tries to connect the dots. Polaris, known as the Guiding Star and the North Star, was used by sailors in ancient times to navigate across Earth's vast seas. He remembers Pytheas of Massalia from the Universal Council's Wiki. A famous Greek explorer credited with being the first man to have sailed from Greece, through the Strait of Gibraltar, to the British Isles, documenting the pagan site Stonehenge as well as Germanic tribes on his travels. This at a time, the first millennia BC, when these lands were green and seas blue. All of, which has since been destroyed by radiation.

'These symbols must depict the voyage of Pytheas. Look how the angle between the sailing boat and Polaris changes on each pictogram', VanWest explains to a by-now disorientated squad.

He continues, 'Look how it sails westwards from our Island, Crete, along what must be the Mediterranean Sea, at a right angle to Polaris... until the last pictogram, an Island directly below Polaris, it must be the British Isles'!

'Heck, it sure does match with the day's theme! Y'all need to take the passage westwards then', Barys concludes.

Each nods in agreement and proceeds with renewed resolve. But, as they veer around the corner, a strange noise, that of demented giggling - *he-he, he-he* - greets them and stops them in their tracks. A blue light, moving towards them, brightens the tunnel ahead. Soon an outline of a man can be seen, the light emanating from his blue laser sword, which he swings wildly from side to side. Kun-lee aims his rifle at the man, VanWest does well to react quickly by grabbing its tip and pulling it down he points at the walls and ceiling. A close call as a blast could have caused a cave-in.

Barys whispers to Kun-lee, 'Make me a clean hit, wait until closer'.

To their dismay, they realise that the man wears blue armour, that of an Enforcer. Except he wears a large unkempt beard, he doesn't look like one of the competitor's from this Games. It's not long before this deranged man is upon them, readying to swoop down with his blade. Kun-lee is first to react, striking him with the butt of his rifle and breaking his neck.

VanWest is sad to see what appears to be a fellow Enforcer killed but, after a short-bewildered pause, he thinks it better to be supportive, 'Good hit'.

'Poor crazy whoever he is', Barys commiserates, also unsure as to what just happened.

'Think... must have breathed in some sensory deprivation gas or something', Kun-lee surmises.

Alpha heckles, 'Maybe he just lost his roach goo at the sight of your ugly face'!

'Nah, was your bad breath that did it', Barys ripostes, exchanging a telling, fed up look with VanWest.

'We need to move on', VanWest recommends, refocusing on the Games. 'There's a race to finish'!

'Better we all take precautions first and activate hazmat mode', Barys suggests, and the squad promptly does so.

'You are smart', Alpha replies sarcastically. 'Any more tips'?

VanWest is sweating profusely, knowing it to be just the start of the dangers listed on the Colonel's list. He wants to take his helmet off to wipe his brow, but his Enforcer training has shown this to be just about the worst thing he could do in such a hostile place.

Before they can fully recompose themselves, as VanWest feared, growling noises - *grr-grr* - cause them to move even more tightly into their defensive square formation. Kun-lee weapon's light shows what appears to be a dog-like creature with large sharp teeth edging closer towards them. Suddenly, it lunges! Barys manages to intercept, swooping down with his laser sword, slicing it in half. However, its death only serves to bring yet more growling - *grr-grr*. More dog-like creatures emerge. And before Alpha can react, one bites down hard into his shoulder - straight through his reinforced titanium armour and energy shield as if it wasn't there at all.

Barys comes to his defence and lops the dog's head clean off, this strike sending the rest of the pack into retreat. Before VanWest can stop him, a wounded and belligerent Alpha swings his rifle round and fires off several disorientated shots. The shots ricochet along the walls, filling the corridor with clouds of dust.

Crack! Stones come crashing to the floor and the passage caves in like falling dominoes in a line.

They try to retreat only for the ground beneath them to collapse, sending them freefalling into the darkness below. Luckily for VanWest, sticky material catches his arms and cushions his fall, stopping him from getting hurt. Slightly shaken but otherwise unharmed, he gets back to his feet. No longer able to resist removing his helmet, he deactivates his hazmat mode and takes it off to catch his breath before convulsing.

Regaining his bearings, he reaches for his amber stone pendant, which to his relief is still tied around his neck, holding it as if to thank it for saving his life. He retrieves his weapon, which lies close by entangled in a bed of sticky silk-like material. Peeling off the threads, the light activates and reveals a network of silky strands. His eyes narrow, to his surprise and dread, he can see that there are bones, human bones and skulls ensnared in it.

VanWest reviews the Colonel's list of dangers, he has encountered quite a few already, *the Packs of mutant dogs* in number 7 check, and numbers *1. Murderous criminals armed with lasers, 2. Booby-traps, fake floors and trip mines, 4. Falling rocks and spikes* and quite possibly *9. Sensory deprivation gases causing hallucinations*, with the maddened man in an Enforcer uniform and beard.

He inspects the area around him - these are neither ordinary skeletons nor themed decorations. A cold shiver runs down his spine. Judging by their armour, albeit of an older design, like the maddened Enforcer they must be contestants of old. Their final foe proving to be too strong for them to overcome. But what number on the list is that? What is this danger?

He dims his weapon's light and cautiously moves forward in search of his squad, trying not to get entangled in the threads. Alpha lies close by, slightly concussed and wincing from his bite wound. He has wrapped his shoulder tightly, making good use of the sticky and silky threads to make a makeshift bandage. VanWest signals to him, placing his index finger on his lips to instruct a dazed Alpha to remain quiet, and then points to the skeletons. VanWest then signals for Alpha to follow as he continues to search for the rest of the squad, Barys and Kun-Lee. At the other end of the passage is a familiar-looking yellow light.

There's another astral map on the floor. And, as with the other one, it appears to depict Pytheas's voyage although at a different point. Here only one pictogram is etched into the stone, that of a long narrow sailing boat docked on an island, what must be the now uninhabitable British Isles with the star Polaris at about 45-degrees to its right. It seems to shine down on the dock. Before he can analyse the drawing further, he notices that his right hand is trembling. Something is amiss!

A low thrum follows, passing along the walls, and a flash crosses his mind. He has a vision of a spider and a trapped Enforcer slowly being eaten alive. He turns his head slightly to his right and freezes. There's an ugly brown creature not too far away, it has not two, not four, but eight long legs. And it does have a body! The creature is meticulously wrapping silk threads around its prey, cocooning it to feast on it later. He's in the lair of every human's nightmare, the most vicious and largest spider of them all, the Gigs Aranea Cavernae Incola. This danger is number 8 on the Colonel's list, gigantic carnivorous insects, in this case, a giant spider.

First discovered in 2535, in Peru, deep underground in a disused mine, this spider is one of only a few lifeforms to excel in an increasingly radioactive world. Having evolved, from a much smaller tarantula, it has grown quite dramatically size-wise! It has since been bred and trained by the Universal Council to hunt and kill rebels hiding deep underground, as well as for entertainment, regularly featuring in executions.

This time, he spots one of the viewing portals, a blob on the ceiling above the spider. Purposely placed there for the Elites and citizens to watch the competitors' grizzly deaths. VanWest is a little taken aback by just how gruesome this spectacle is, likely made to show a heroic death by a giant spider, in truth terribly cruel. In the midst of such danger, a fleeting thought crosses his mind, how most of those of low odds are being used, the prize so unattainable. But as an Enforcer, he cannot question and think these devious thoughts about his masters. And, he realises that this wrapped body could be one of his missing squad members. He must take action to help!

Alpha, now able to talk, whispers, 'We need to get out... Let's go'.

'Over there, that could be Barys and Kun-lee. We are a squad, we fight and die together. There is honour, we cannot leave without them', VanWest objects in a low voice.

'Roach them! There's a race on, and time is running out. Let's go, that's an order'! Alpha only thinking of the prize, HIS prize.

VanWest pushes Alpha's hand away as he attempts to pull him along. Unfortunately, the commotion catches the attention of the spider. It swiftly turns towards them - *screech* - as if angered by the interruption to its feasting preparations. VanWest reacts fast by firing his weapon, which pierces the creature's abdomen, splashing green goo across. Despite this, the spider remains upright, now even more incensed. Its spindly and razor-sharp front legs kick out at him, knocking him to the floor and his rifle in the opposite direction. Alpha jumps out of the way and flees. His cowardly run does not evade the spider's wrath; it catches him with an ejection of gooey sticky thread, pinning him against the adjacent wall.

Lying winded on his back, VanWest watches as the creature crawls over him. Its pinchers opening wide as it leers, salivating as if imagining him to be a tantalising and bloodied piece of raw tartare. VanWest is paralysed, frozen in fear, envisioning his body being put into a moribund state as his blood is slowly sucked out. He never imagined going out this way.

All seems lost as the spider's pinchers bear down on him, but then a blue light illuminates the lair. The light swoops down from above, cutting the spider's head clean off. To his relief, he finds it belongs to that of a Blue team Enforcer... Barys! His distinct purple eyes instantly recognisable. Barys cuts the spider's legs next, splattering more goo across as it collapses and slams against the floor. It is dead.

Clearing the saliva and goo from VanWest's face and armour, Barys stretches out his hand and pulls him to his feet, exchanging a salute and a smile.

'Barys, you saved my life! I will repay you one day. As per the code of honour, you can ask me any favour'.

'No problem, VanWest. There is always honour between us... where's Kun'?

'I saw the spider threading a cocoon... there, over there'! VanWest points.

Barys sets about cutting through the silk threads with his laser sword, finally uncovering Kun-lee's deathly pale face, allowing him to breathe freely. VanWest leans over, placing two fingers on his neck, he detects a faint pulse. Relieved, he goes somewhat reluctantly to Alpha, who is still stuck against the wall and pulls him from the gooey, sticky matter. He focuses once again on the squad's objective: to help the Blue team win, and yes, even if it means that Alpha is the one collecting its ultimate prize of Elite status.

'Give us a hand to lift up Kun', Barys asks, not quite realising the full extent of Alpha's injury.

'Roach him! Let's go! We don't have time', Alpha responds in an irritated tone, quickly remaking his silk bandage.

'Alpha, you see me leaving you behind? Gosh, saved you twice already. Where's your sense of duty and honour at'? Barys berates him while lifting Kun-lee's limp body over his shoulders.

'The competition isn't about honour, it is about winning. Kun is going to make us lose'! Alpha counters. Barys shakes his head in disgust and looks away.

Determined to escape this maze, VanWest returns to the dimly lit astral map. His eyes focusing once again on the boat that is docking, wondering why its journey ends in line with the star Polaris. The star seems to shine brightest. Wanting to see it better, he asks the squad to 'turn-off' their weapon's light. *Eureka!* There's a promising discovery, in the dark he can see a faint stream of light cutting through the dock and Polaris at a 45-degree angle and radiating out of the map.

VanWest follows the light stream to its source, the others following curiously, whilst also staying wary of any other danger that could lie ahead. After several steps, they find that it originates from a very tiny slit in the rocks, there is a loose stone. VanWest bends down to pull it free from the wall, after several forceful yanks opens it up, sending a flood of light into the hallway. It's a path to the surface!

Opening up the orifice as wide as possible, VanWest keeps his honour by helping Barys to drag Kun-lee through. An impatient Alpha standing guard behind. One after the other they squeeze through and exit. They have completed the voyage as indicated on the astral map, reaching the end of the *Pytheas's Labyrinth.*

As they exit, a deafening cacophony of explosions and warning sirens ring out. Their communicators also reactivate. The exasperated voice of their base commander, the Colonel, comes through, 'Enforcers! Are your cerebral hearing implants working? Copy that? ... Answer'!

'Affirmative, Colonel! Communicators working', VanWest is the first to reply.

'Affirmative, Colonel'! Alpha and Barys both reply next.

'Enforcers, you are behind. Separate if you must and roaching sprint to the orange light. The Reds are winning the race... Remember to stay sharp, these Space Roaches will be up to all sorts of dirty tricks. I warn you too, if you can't run you better wait for a medical bot. Copy that'?

'Roger that, Colonel'! They confirm.

Pytheas's Labyrinth has taken a hefty toll. The Colonel needs them to win the race. But they can no longer go as a squad of four, VanWest looks at Kun-lee, whose lips have turned a frosty blue, his body showing all the symptoms of anaphylactic shock. And then looks at Alpha, whose wound has bled through his makeshift web bandage, he looks pale and greatly enervated.

Barys and VanWest can ill afford to support their weaker colleagues. They will need all their strength and energy to finish and survive this final stage. The orange light from the gateway into Stage 3, *the Fire of Vesta*, calls them on. A stage that promises to be the sternest test. If Stage 2 is about teamwork, Stage 3 is about individuals seeking a prize that many would literally kill for!

Their emergence from the caves has seen the leaderboard update, their images prompting rapturous applause. After just two hours of racing, they find that the maze has recorded its highest casualty rate ever recorded, only *21 Out Of The 200 Competitors Remain. 179* are listed as *Inactive*, including Kun-lee. An instruction rolls through VanWest's Moggle X lenses, informing him that *00:04:00 Remain To Complete Stage 2* before disqualification.

VanWest urges an injured Alpha to capitulate and help Kun-lee, 'You better wait for a medical bot to arrive. You are not strong enough for the *Fires* of Vesta, stay, make sure Kun gets medical attention'.

Alpha grunts angrily, 'You think I can't handle a bit of pain? Roachtard, I'm here to win. He's a dead man... Dump him and let's go'!

'Have some honour! You owe me to make sure he gets out of here'! Barys calls honour on him, having rescued Alpha twice.

Attempting to continue forward, Alpha half faints and stumbles back. Seeing his oily blood running down his arm and dripping from his hand, he finally realises that his Games is over, 'Roaching Hell'!

Barys lays Kun-lee's limp body down beside him, 'Remember the code of honour, get him out'!

Begrudgingly capitulating, Alpha cannot stop himself from taking a final parting shot, showing his true colours once more, 'You roachtards are screwed without me. You aren't Elite material. The Reds have already won'!

VanWest shrugs his shoulders, there's no time to waste on Alpha's spiteful words. Resolutely, he hurries up the slope alongside Barys towards the orange light. Without a moment to spare, they enter together into the final stage, the *Fires of Vesta*.

Chapter 3 Forewarned

A surreal scene greets them, fire shooting up from pits and boulders crashing down from the sky. The collision of the rocks and fire produces layer upon layer of thick dust, making the white light of the finish line faint and distant like that of a faraway star. The air is hostile to breathe; putrid and acidic, it forces Barys and VanWest to activate their hazmat masks. A few minutes more of this and their lungs would burn, bringing with it a painful death.

The *Fires of Vesta* looks to be a near-exact copy of last year's final stage. Fortunately, the Blues have trained well for this under the Colonel's tutelage. Barys and VanWest might even have a fighting chance of finishing. Notwithstanding this, their endurance and agility, including the ability to duck, run and jump as well as dive at a split-second's notice, will be most certainly tested.

As the Colonel has warned them, it could also prove to be a test of cunning. The Red team's Space Roaches are undoubtedly lurking in blind spots. The high number of canyons scattered across this course are ideal for hiding and laying ambushes. Both would be wise to remain ready for the unexpected!

VanWest and Barys check their communicators for any new instructions, only to find that they have been deactivated once more. They use their Moggle X mapping system to plot their route forward, calibrating it to return an optimal risk-reward path that will take them around the most dangerous parts of the debris field, *North-East 44-Degrees, Fatality Risk 40%, Finish Time 00:20:00.*

Except they quickly realise that they don't actually have 20 minutes, that is if they want to win. Looking up at the leaderboard, a Red Space Soldier is much further ahead than previously thought, his lead nearly insurmountable. If they want to bring the honour home for the Blues and win this race, there is only one choice to make, to re-calibrate their Moggle Xs for a more dangerous route. Barys and VanWest exchange a look and decide to go for it!

Their Moggle Xs return with a route that takes them straight through the boulder canyon, *North 0 Degrees, Fatality Risk 90%, Finish Time 00:15:00*. More than doubling their risk of death.

Agreeing, they charge into the fray following its path. Ducking to avoid the sharp-edged boulders raining down and jumping over flames that lash violently up at them and singes their armour and boots. In hindsight, their choice of plasma rifle over a jetpack may have proven to be somewhat short-sighted. As rookies, they hadn't really planned to make it this far. Even though the debris field grows denser and the fire more violent, they skilfully keep progressing onwards against the odds.

As Barys manages to avoid yet another roving boulder, VanWest isn't so lucky. *Clank!* A piece of debris breaks away and clips his shoulder, deactivating his energy shield and throwing his plasma rifle out of reach. Barys rushes over to help, grabbing his arm and signalling for them to leap down into the canyon below, to take shelter from another fast approaching boulder. With no time to spare, they jump and land on a pile of smouldering gravel onto a ground littered with fragments of red and blue armour.

'I have a bad feeling, we shouldn't have come down here', VanWest warns Barys, pointing to the fragments. His hands tremble, similar to the Spider's lair.

'Relax VanWest. Look a support cache'! Barys points enthusiastically towards a red box on top of a large pile of rocks opposite them.

VanWest spots a red light. Knowing it to be danger, he screams 'Red'! But it's too late, several shots are already hurtling towards them.

Whilst it's technically against the rules to attack fellow competitors, this canyon is a viewing blind spot, effectively making it a no holds barred battleground. One of the shots deflects off a rock and catches Barys, piercing his body armour and ripping his torso open. His energy shield and hazmat gear knocked out of action and no longer able to protect him. He falls to his knees shrieking in agony, the acidic air entering his body, quickly turning his purple eyes yellowish as his blood boils. VanWest attempts to grab Barys's plasma rifle to return fire, but another flurry of shots from the Soldier's rifle incinerates the weapon before he can take hold of it.

With the rifle now training on him, VanWest ducks down and scrambles towards the support cache, doing his best to avoid the debris and boulders that fall from above. The rifle's shots narrowly miss him, and somehow he manages to reach the cache. As he grabs hold of the proton energy net inside, the Space Soldier, having activated his jetpack, lands right on top of him delivering a crushing kick to his ribs, which sends VanWest tumbling back under a plume of dust.

VanWest recognises the *Cr* symbol on his red shoulder plate, it's Major Chromes! The Space Army's poster boy and last year's runner up to its champion, Lt. Colonel Omega. Colonel Cornelius forewarned them about the 'Space Roaches', and their 'dirty tricks' - these competitors are without honour. In hindsight, both him and Barys should have taken heed and been warier when plotting their route.

VanWest thinks fast, using the wall of dust to his advantage, he takes a risky gamble to remove the exterior layer of his body armour in order to make a decoy. He hopes to lure his dangerous foe into a surprise attack of his own. With only a thin layer of protective clothing to guard against the acidic air and any plasma shot, he hurries to hide behind a large rock before the dust settles. His armour shimmers, speckles of light breaking through the dust, enticing an oblivious Chromes in.

'Got no skill, so very easy! Ha-ha'! Chromes taunts as he discharges several shots into the armour. But as soon as the words leave his mouth, he realises that he has made a crucial mistake, for this is a training class plasma rifle and not a combat one. He has unwittingly temporarily emptied his rifle's charge.

Seeing that his trap has worked, VanWest leaps from behind the rocks and counterattacks, throwing his proton energy net over a surprised Chromes.

'Barys has a message for you, he says to go roach yourself', VanWest yells as he tightens the proton energy net, suffocating Chromes until he passes out. The net designed to protect against debris proves to be an effective weapon as well.

Bittersweet, he has made some progress. The announcer updates that only 'Two Red Soldiers' and 'One Blue Enforcer' remain. He's the only Blue Enforcer left! This stage proving to be as deadly as the last. The smog above him dissipates as his face projects across the dome, those in the stands rapturously applauding. VanWest takes a deep breath through his hazmat mask, there is no time to celebrate. The leaderboard also shows that the two Red Soldiers are much closer to the finish line than him. The fight with Chromes has not only severely wounded Barys but has also cost him valuable time, time that he could ill afford to lose.

He races over to a now unconscious Barys, grabbing his damaged blue armour on the way and placing it over his open wound. He manages to reactivate the hazmat mode, which to his relief still partially works. Despite wanting to stay and make sure his friend is okay, he knows all would have been in vain if the Red team were to win today. By giving him the body armour, he has hopefully saved his life and thus repaid the code of honour he owes. Barys should be picked up later. Well, at least VanWest convinces himself that he will be.

An evermore VanWest opens his Moggle X to map out a new shortcut, re-calibrating its settings to give him a faster finishing time. It returns a shorter path, albeit with an extremely high possibility of death, *Fatality Risk 95%, 00:11:00*. But it still too much time if he wants to win! He's going to need an upgrade.

His skirmish may not have been entirely fruitless, he rips Chromes's sleek jetpack from his shoulders. It could shave off ten whole minutes. His Moggle X automatically re-calibrates as he throws it over his shoulders, showing *Fatality Risk 95%, 00:01:00*. He could still win but it would be a miracle. Undeterred, he switches the controls to manual and powers forward.

Thrusting the joystick from side to side, he accelerates through the dense debris field, adroitly manoeuvring around each rock with his quick reactions. His mind is now purely focused on keeping the Games trophy from the Red team's Space Soldiers. HE MUST WIN!

Despite the white wall of light, the finish line being so close, his luck could have finally run out as a rock fragment catches - *thwack* - the back of his helmet, throwing his head violently forward. The superior composition of the Hubert family-sponsored helmet saving him from decapitation, he can feel moisture trickling down his neck. His eyes start to narrow, and his vision blurs, with the jetpack still propelling him forward he drifts into unconsciousness.

VanWest finds himself in a lab in an incubator labelled *Van der Westhuizen, A1*, where a bald man with big green eyes smiles down at him. The shaking of a rattle causes him to chuckle loudly, but the light starts to fade.

He finds himself somewhere new, sitting on a purple mat in a large white room, rolling a blue plastic ball back and forth with a toddler. The same bald-headed man from before, wearing the same white lab coat, catches the ball. There's an electroneedle in his hands, still smiling, he comes over to take VanWest's arm, pricking it as he shuts his eyes and screams.

Re-opening them, he is now under a stairwell gazing happily at a young girl, she can be no more than 12 years old. Her eyes a piercing electric blue and her hair frizzy and jet-black, she leans over to give him a peck on the cheek but a loud - *creak* - stops them still. Her smile disappears, hurriedly she gives him a big hug before the door slides open. An angry grey-haired woman dressed in a blue matron uniform scowls at them before pulling the girl out by her ear. The girl screams and tries to resist, kicking and punching in an attempt to getaway but cannot. In the commotion, her necklace snaps and her pendant falls to the floor. He tries to give chase, but as he does so, an intense white light replaces the scene.

The room changes to something quite alien and not of this time: there's a conference room with rows of tables covered in white cloth and a bunch of men dressed in what must be mid-20th-century style business suits, listening intensely into bulky headsets that cover their ears. In front of the men are flags belonging to long dissolved nations, most prominent is the one with a white cross against a red background.

The scene changes dramatically once again, to that of a white sandy beach. A wondrous sight, the moon's light refracts off crystal blue waves that crash along the shoreline.

But it does not last long, the sound of the waves replaced by another noise, his name 'VanWest' chanted over and over, it crescendos until he awakens back on the course. He has drifted back into consciousness.

He looks around in disbelief, somehow he has survived the debris field and is only meters away from the finish line. The shortcut has worked. The Red Space Soldier now trails too far behind to catch up.

The announcer hails his arrival with an equal level of disbelief and excitement, 'Citizens! Citizens! A first-time entrant with starting odds of 150-1, yes 150-1, is on course to be the winner of the Universal Games' trophy. Praise the Universal! Never in the history of the Games has this happened. Praise the Universal'!

'Salve the Universal'! The citizens hail.

In front of VanWest is victory and the zenith of any Enforcer's career: Elite status. As he approaches the home straight, his image broadcasts triumphantly from the surrounding holoscreens. Enchanting young women dressed in Roman tunics, their red and blonde hair braided in cornrows, shower him with real flower petals, so very rare in the year 3000, a befitting gift.

The captivating women are meant to be the Vestal virgin priestesses, guardians of the fire of Vesta, the Goddess of the Hearth and Home in Roman times. A virgin God dedicated to serving the God of Jupiter, as seen in the statue at the start of the course. For the Universal Council, she represents domestic tranquillity and servitude. A homemaker that keeps society in balance and an important example for its female citizens to follow.

The priestesses' flower petals float around him as he passes through the white light, welcoming him into a large rococo chamber adorned with Romanesque granite statues of old and new Universal Council members. VanWest has arrived at the temple known as *Universalis Domum de Praeterito,* the chamber of the Universal Council.

'Welcome, VanWest'!

The citizens go silent as a bald man, with a long white goatee and dark brown eyes appears on the stage. He is dressed in a shimmering opal toga and wears a golden leafed corona. VanWest recognises him instantly, it is the highest-ranking Elite of them all, the immortal Head of the Universal Council, Dr King. He holds aloft an ornate red and blue coloured trophy that is spherical in shape. It is inscribed with the Enforcer motto and the second commandment, *Pro Progressio Hominis et Universales.*

A loud cheer breaks the silence as the surrounding walls shift and four Elites step forward, men that VanWest knows all too well. Four-star General Vladimir of the Space Army, Dr Minus Schuurman the Head of Science, Commissioner Ming the Head of the Police Forces, the Enforcers and Inspectors, and the Blue team's base commander, Colonel Cornelius. The Colonel looks immensely pleased, and definitely a little surprised.

They stand proudly with their chins high, each wrapped in their own ceremonial toga and green-leafed corona. VanWest instinctively responds to his masters with a low bow, deferring to them his utmost respect and subservience.

Tooo-tooo-tooo-toom! Conical bronze tubas play a low-pitched sound, signalling for all those watching to quieten down as Dr King steps forward, 'Captain VanWest, congratulations on your marvellous achievement. Lest I need to say, you have beaten the odds and shown incredible strength and resolve. Your win is for the progression of man and the Universal. And I, therefore, present to you the greatest prize, the Universal Red and Blue Games Trophy'.

After a small pause, he instructs, 'Remove your helmet and hold the trophy high, in the name of the Universal. All praise'!

Prompting the citizens to respond, once again, 'Salve the Universal'!

VanWest removes his helmet only to find his hands covered in blood. Nevertheless, he takes the trophy from Dr King. But, as he tries to lift it up, his vision begins to blur and the room to spin. *Clank!* It falls from his hands as he loses his footing and collapses onto the marble floor, unconscious. The floor is no longer marble; the white sand has returned. Before him is the shoreline and wondrous blue sea. A shiny object lies not too far away, refracting the moon's light. Partly covered, it seems out of place, compelling him to pull it out. It's a large sheet of metal, charred at its tip. Wiping away the sand grains, he finds the letters *ENDEA*. As he tries to make sense of it, a heavy gust of wind blows through.

The wind sucks up the sand, lifting it up like a tornado to unmask a structure beneath, a charred and twisted wreck with small black wings on each side. There's a peculiar smell of burning rubber and metal. Covering his face instinctively, smoke starts to rise from within. Suddenly flames shoot out, engulfing the wreck and turning it into a raging inferno. Howls of pain follow, accompanied by loud pounding, the chilling sound of human fists slamming against metal. The noise and flames dissipate as quickly as they came.

Replacing it with an even more horrific sight, that of badly burnt bodies. The frizzy jet-black haired woman from earlier is there too, she kneels beside them, her face obscured. Her hair is similar also to that of the little girl under the stairs. The woman holds a circular device, it's an old type of Corrupter, a long-banned tool used by rebels to, as the name suggests, corrupt electronic equipment.

Waaahhhh! A siren blares, two vehicles are fast approaching, red coloured fire engines not of the year 3000, they belong to another time: the late 20th century. The bright white light returns and causes him to shield his eyes once more. Re-opening them, the wreck and fire engines are gone, replaced by an altogether different scene, with it a feeling of calm and happiness.

He stands on a deck overlooking the water, the frizzy-haired woman is there. Her face still obscured, she gently rows a wooden boat towards him. In his arms, he finds himself holding a small child, who waves enthusiastically at the woman. She waves back but then the scene fades. A voice calls out his name 'VanWest, VanWest... wake up, wake up'.

Chapter 4 The Doctor Knows

VanWest rouses from his sleep. His head heavy and numb, he knows not if he is still dreaming. Across the windowless room, the prettiest woman he has ever seen stares at him intensely. Her eyes a most captivating electric blue, her hair frizzy and jet black. On her index finger is a bluish-green emerald ring and she wears a nurse's uniform with a circular nametag: *Universal Nurse Rose*.

'Hello VanWest'! She welcomes him warmly as if greeting a long-lost friend. Calling forward a silver-plated medical robot, who rumbles towards his bed, rhythmically beeping, to present a flat stainless-steel tray filled with multi-coloured capsules.

Attempting to sit up, he finds himself held back by the straps tied around his bruised wrists. Looking at Nurse Rose in confusion, she points to the ceiling above him. He's connected to a Schuurman Reporter Monitor (SRM). Unlike conventional hospital monitors, it does more than just observe one's vital signs - it reads one's memories and thoughts. Originally designed to aid medical staff in nursing their patients back to health, the Universal Council's Inspectors have long since used the SMR for a much darker purpose. Not only to interrogate prisoners, but too their own forces, to check that their Enforcers' minds remain uncorrupted and free of devious thoughts.

For this reason, many Enforcers fear to get injured as it often results in them being assigned a prolonged stay in a re-educational institute. Seeing this, VanWest starts to realise he is no longer dreaming, this is all very real.

He asks her, in a stutter, 'Where am I... I'?

Looking over her shoulder, the answer is right in front of him, in large black letters a sign reads *Rehabilitation Ward B*. In a clearer voice he asks another question, 'Ward B. Why am I here'?

'Please relax. You have been in and out of consciousness, only waking to make claims. Claims about', she stops herself from explaining further.

The woman deactivates the SMR, before adding, 'You were transferred here for recovery'. She then takes a few blue capsules from the tray and dissolves them in a beaker of water, and loosens his restraints.

VanWest has heard enough disturbing tales about Ward B to know that this is not just a re-education and rehabilitation ward. There are stories of the Universal Council sending officials, academics, and others deemed delusional here for 'rehabilitation' only to not be seen again. The most notorious of being the Elite and former Head of Science for the Universal Council, Dr Isaac VonHelmann. Sent for observation on the grounds of insanity, earning him the moniker 'Mad Newton'.

One of only a few to have left Ward B, Barys once told him in confidence, that he left, well escaped, unaided from this place. The Universal Council reported a very different take at the time: a deviant cult called the Utopians had kidnapped him, doing unspeakable acts to convert him to their crazy religion, and brainwashed him.

Ward B is very secluded, situated inside a forbidden for Enforcers section of the Asclepius medical complex. One of the four main areas of the Universal Council's moon base - the others being the Enforcer academy, the Universal Senate offices and Schuurman's Research lab, the latter also forbidden to Enforcers. On the moon, there are few human settlements with the nearest civilisation located at the small domed trading post called Clavius Crater, some 500 miles away. Purposely built to be far-removed from Antarctica's citizens, it serves as a well-isolated place for members of the Universal Council to meet. All those within carefully monitored.

Helping VanWest to take a sip and swallow a capsule, what she says next startles him. 'This should help hide what I am about to tell you'.

'Hide'!? VanWest asks her with a perplexed look, Universal personnel do not hide anything. For him, the deactivating of an SRM and this word 'hide' is alarming, these are displays of abnormal and deviant behaviour.

The nurse switches the holoscreen on, which automatically plays its only channel, a propaganda piece on the Universal Red and Blue Games. It's showing Dr King parading the trophy with blue confetti lights flickering all around. The citizens cheer as he holds a man's arm aloft on the parade float. But there is something very creepy about it.

'What'!? A shocked VanWest sees that this man looks just like himself. It IS him! The man is wearing a blue ceremonial toga, triumphantly waving and shouting the same word over and over again, 'Universal, Universal, Universal'!

VanWest rubs his eyes in disbelief, he says aloud, 'This cannot be me'!

He doesn't recall being there. The location, listed in the bottom right-hand corner, *Queen Elizabeth, Antarctic*, is a place that he has never even visited before. He has never even been to the capital!

In the year 3000, Queen Elizabeth is Earth's most populous settlement. This once British territory's name originates from the early 21st century, to honour their then longest-reigning and much-loved monarch Queen Elizabeth II. For once upon a time this land was an unpolluted icy world, pristine and void of humans, teeming with fish stocks. This land, twice the size of their home, the United Kingdom, became a magnet for waves of immigrants as continents nearer the equator became uninhabitable. It reached its peak population by the 25th century.

Much cooler and less polluted at the time, Antarctica was the only place where humans could survive above ground, at least for long periods. With the rise of the Universal Council, the United Kingdom ceded sovereignty. Nevertheless, its history and accomplishments remain remembered and even revered. So much so that Dr King choose not to change its name.

With the Universal Red and Blue Games serving as an important propaganda tool, a showcase of the Universal Council's might, this parade could not be missed. It would be an ignominious event, a humiliation if so. It would not be too farfetched that a stand-in, a visual trick has been used to make the citizens believe it was actually him there.

'Is that me'? VanWest quizzes the nurse.

Before she can answer, the room starts to shake, there must be a ship landing. Its vibrations are so strong it causes the robot's tray to drop, spilling and scattering the remaining multi-coloured capsules across the concrete floor.

Nurse Rose goes slightly pale, her forehead frowning as she hurries to lock the metal door, turning to warn him, 'They are watching, you are never alone. Your memories of the past, the truth, have been blocked, tampered with. VanWest, the Universal Council is evil. They have and will lie to you, use you, and then destroy you'.

'What do you mean? Who are you'? He asks bewildered.

'VanWest, they must not know our conversation took place, do not let them into your mind. Block them! Otherwise, our lives will be in danger. For many years, we tried to protect you, but this evil now knows too much'.

'Have we met before? ... I feel we have, who are you'? He asks her desperately.

The woman wraps her soft and long-fingered hand around his pendant and leans over to give him a peck on his forehead, her lips warm and soft, leaving a faint smell of lavender perfume over him.

She edges towards the holoscreen, which changes to black and whispers a poem.

> "Hope" is the thing with feathers -
> That perches in the soul -
> And sings the tune without the words -
> And never stops - at all

Boom! There's a knock on the door. Placing her hand inside the screen, she glazes back at him lovingly, mouthing the words 'Till we meet again'.

Boom! There's another heavy thump against the locked door as she disappears inside. *Boom!* A third, heavier, knock unlocks the door and throws it wide open. A large man in a dark black Enforcer uniform and black peaked cap marches in. It is his base commander, the Elite Colonel Cornelius! Two-armed patrol androids follow the Colonel through the door, their faces even less human-like than those of the Space Soldiers, bearing synthetic skin and beady stolid eyes. These Elite patrol androids make no pretence of being human. Their strange metallic arms double up as heavy elongated plasma guns, they reach to twice their own height. More advanced models than those found in the settlements, they only serve the top Elites and the Universal Council.

'Captain VanWest, our monitor detected that you had awoken. Perfect timing for there is an important meeting for us to attend', the Colonel informs him seemingly oblivious that Nurse Rose was just here.

Never one for pleasantries and before VanWest can reply, one of the patrol androids marches over to his bed, breaking his constraints before brutishly throwing him to the floor by his ankles. Only to then lift him back to his feet and lead him, dressed in his medical gown, into a long cold corridor. He's barefoot, virtually naked, and void of his bionic upgrades. The only item his own is tied around his neck, his amber stone pendant.

He follows the Colonel past a series of mirrored panels, each of, which reflects his own dishevelled appearance - a scruffy, unshaven man with bloodshot grey eyes. The hall is nearly pitch-black except for the dim glow of the security lights. His mind races as he ponders his fate, wary of what lies at the end of this lowly lit and eerily quiet corridor.

As he continues walking, he reaches a flashing neon sign Surgical Unit and turns into a hallway filled with panels that change colour as they pass by. Dark shadows seem to move from behind - VanWest notices on each a four-digit Enforcer identification code. Shocked stops still at one in particular, this is a code he knows well. The opaque red of this panel begins to fade as he takes a step forward, revealing a man suspended in a liquid medium. His arms, torso and head are connected to dozens of cables. There's a large scar on the man's torso. It is in the exact place where Barys was shot in Stage 3 of the Games. Could it be him!?

VanWest presses his palm against the panel, causing the man's eyes to open wide. The man IS Barys! The pupils of his purple eyes now fully dilated and body lifeless. At least they are no longer yellow. One of the androids loses patience and pushes him forward, causing the panel to turn opaque red once again.

The silver metal door at the end of the corridor automatically slides open to reveal a magnificent vessel perched on a rock: the Elite transport ship called the SCC-400. The large streamlined spaceship stands imposingly. A striking blue colour, it reaches up over 250 feet high and 400 meters wide. Its bow points upwards like a pointy beak, and its stern is weighed down by two huge warp thrusters, which stick out on either side.

The androids flank him as he walks behind the Colonel, escorting him up a shiny metal docking ramp before coming to an abrupt halt outside the ship's entrance. For several minutes VanWest waits, doing his best to remain stolid, his thoughts are filled with trepidation, not knowing what will happen next. Worried too at seeing Barys in such a state. Two possible scenarios lie ahead. The first, a promotion to Elite status, the second, quite the opposite: something more sinister and perhaps fatal. Suddenly, a bolt of green light shoots down and transports him inside.

He arrives in front of a yellow neon sign that reads *Elites Quarters*. Now on the upper deck of the ship, this is an area usually forbidden to Enforcers where only Elites are permitted to enter. He hopes this to be a good sign, with the androids gone the Colonel now ushers him forward. However, he wonders why he hasn't been made to change first, why is this so urgent!?

The only item in the corridor is a large blue NASA Meatball logo, composed of a sphere, orbit, red chevron, and stars, the plaque underneath reads *Alpha Mission Control, Space Kennedy 2000*. As he looks at it, the logo disappears and transforms into a room. In the middle are two men, their backs turned to the door, who stand deep in concentration absorbed by a small holographic map, a 4D holomap. Marking various points as it turns, they cross out numerous places with a red mark, one of, which is ColaBeers. Places he knows were once sites of unrest and high NEA activity.

As the Colonel steps inside, the holomap stops spinning at Queen Elizabeth, Antarctica. With a respectful bow, he greets them, 'My liege, sorry for this interruption. Your guest, Captain VanWest, has arrived'.

Turning around, the bald man with a white goatee is none other than Dr King himself, the Head of the Universal Council. The other man, with his distinctive black unibrow and near Cyclops eyes, is Commissioner Ming, Head of the Police Forces. His shiny bluish-black imperial uniform similar to that of the Colonel.

Taken aback at finding the two highest-ranking members of the Universal Council before him, his jaw drops briefly. Quick to regain his composure, he bows several times subserviently to his masters, his liege, Dr King. An Enforcer of his rank is not permitted to directly address Elites without permission. Thus, he obsequiously stares down at the floor.

Dr King is known to only make grand public appearances at special events such as the Universal Red and Blue Games. In many ways he's quite aloof; few Enforcers ever met him one-on-one. However, star-struck wouldn't be the right term to use in this circumstance, a better word would be petrified!

'I gather that you are wondering why we have summoned you here, my boy'? Dr King speaks.

'Yes, my liege', VanWest responds in a low cracking voice, a little surprised to be addressed as if they are familiar, using this word 'boy'.

'My boy... Lest I must say, your great victory in the Universal Games has earned you recognition, the possibility of its most esteemed prize, one every Enforcer dreams of, to be a higher being - an Elite - and closer to the Universal'.

VanWest looks up slightly, hoping that the first of the possible scenarios is coming true. The thought of standing beside the Elites as a Lt. Colonel fills his mind.

Dr King changes tone, 'This Captain VanWest... this cannot happen now'.

'But...' VanWest just about stops himself. Bowing obsequiously several times, knowing it to be an offence to question his superior, 'Apologies, my liege'.

Dr King scowls at him, not pleased by his interruption, 'Do not forget yourself, Enforcer! We have serious matters to discuss, for there is something more serious on the horizon'.

'Apologies, my liege', he bows again even lower.

Dr King then steps closer. His eyes stare suspiciously into his, their noses nearly touching, 'Lest I need not say... you already know this, correct'?

A baffled VanWest shakes his head, he racks his brains for a possible explanation, but he cannot think of anything. His response just pure bewilderment and silence.

Dr King waits several long seconds, before raising his voice, 'ENDEA..., don't look so puzzled boy! You know that the Universal Council is all-knowing'!

VanWest takes a step back, his hands trembling, he tries to explain himself, 'My liege, it was a dream. I apologise but it wasn't real. A dream, nothing more'!

Dr King's eyes continue to narrow, 'No, VanWest! It wasn't... Tell me about it'!

'Apologies, my liege. Just a random dream, I do not know of what'!? VanWest pleads.

Even though it is not surprising that Dr King could have seen his dreams, VanWest is shocked that this could be treated as anything but fantasy. Now fearing that the second of the two possible scenarios is coming true, the Council does not take kindly to peculiarities in their Enforcers. Nurse Rose deactivated the SRM, he wonders again why she was there to 'protect' him? Trying to hide his thoughts?

Dr King's tone changes, less accusatory, 'Lest we had not known your gift but the race and your injury showed us... A gift bestowed on you to help further the progression of man and the Universal... Do you understand'?

The Universal Council knows about his ability to see ahead. This 'gift', not one he can control and rather random in nature. It has helped him many times as an Enforcer. Indeed, his promotion to Captain was thanks to this, his capture of a NEA rebel leader in ColaBeers when he foresaw her ambush.

After her brutal torture at the hands of an Inspector, 'the Interrogator', she divulged her secret NEA base locations. Information used to destroy the rebel's headquarters hidden under a number of densely populated slums. And, with it, the massacre of thousands of innocent citizens who resided above. The deathly screams of which still haunt him. Men, women and children who knew nothing of the NEA's comings and goings, their only crime being in the wrong place at the wrong time. It was his job to remove all traces of the atrocity, to ensure that the citizens never would speak of it. His conscience too weak, too scared to challenge his superiors. The Universal Council is all-knowing and sacrosanct, the Enforcers duty-bound to follow them. Their motto and the second commandment, to work for the progression of man and the Universal, justified it all.

Commissioner Ming interjects respectfully, 'Dr King if I may... Captain VanWest, the Universal Council of the past, would have deemed your ability that of a deviant, an abomination, but your creation had reason. Your psychic abilities are a tool for us, the Universal Council, to stop what you have seen'.

'Commissioner, apologies, "creation" '? He replies, his voice hoarse and head still bowed, he cannot understand why he has been called a 'creation'.

The Commissioner doesn't answer his question, side-stepping, he asks, 'Captain VanWest, you know well the deviants known as the Utopians, yes'?

'Of course, a scourge', VanWest replies.

'Yes! Be sure these religious extremists, anti-technology anarchists and ultra-environmentalists are readying to bring us back into the dark ages. They have spread like a plague through our settlements, taking advantage of weak-minded citizens'.

'Yes, Commissioner. Very much so', VanWest replies in agreement.

The Commissioner continues, 'Your vision of a 20th-century conference room over a millennia ago corresponds to a piece of intelligence we recently acquired about their next mission. A most alarming piece. It could spell the end of our present, our magnificent world, with all progression lost'!

'It can... cannot be so', VanWest replies, his voice breaking. Astounded to hear that this could be anything more than just a weird dream!?

'Watch this'! The Commissioner points to the holomap.

An interface, tagged *History 101*, commences. It features the once Head of Science, and now well-known traitor of the Universal Council, Mad Newton. A quantum mechanics physicist who invented the Magicbox, the precursor to all transporters, and many other technologies.

The holomap interfaces with his cerebral cortex, focusing in on Mad Newton's last project and a shocking revelation.

In 2991, Dr Isaac VonHelmann, later to become Mad Newton, invented the rod-shaped Quantum Accelerator, the next giant leap for humankind - Time-travel. During testing, he sent numerous lab-engineered chimpanzees to pre-selected times and locations on Earth, which were programmed into their short-term memory. The results were mixed, with many chimpanzees not rematerialising where and when expected, leading to the cancellation of further tests. Another failure could have been catastrophic, severely changing time and with it the present. Slight changes to history were detected from the first tests, including a news report in 2212 of a chimpanzee materialising at the inauguration of US President Gustavo Gonzales, and another in 2012 at the Diamond Jubilee concert held for Queen Elizabeth II in London.

The Commissioner's forehead wrinkles as he explains the very worrying connection to their intelligence, 'Concealing it from us... Mad Newton built a second rod-shaped Quantum Accelerator. Hell-bent on taking us back to the dark ages of the late 20th century, he seeks to destroy all the progression of man and the Universal'.

Dr King exchanges a look with the Commissioner, 'The Universal is all-knowing. Lest I must say, do not fear, we have the time and place of where he seeks to commit this most heinous of acts. 1951, in a once large city called Paris, the City of Lights. Tell me what you saw of this place, the desks'?

VanWest does not know how to reply, he struggles to comprehend. Time travel? 1951? Paris?

Dr King huffs, 'Boy! You would do well to reply... For your vision shows us a conference room with white clothed tables, this could be a place of an important meeting. Understand'?

Dr King, seeing VanWest's struggle, decides to pause, changing to a friendlier tone, 'My boy, enough for now. You must prepare yourself. Be ready for this place'.

VanWest gasps, 'Excuse me, my liege... this place'?!

Dr King frowns, but gives him the details, 'Listen, boy! 1951 Paris! Preparations on Earth will commence at zero five hundred. Special training for time travel, the Colonel will help you prepare... That is all for now'.

A bewildered VanWest takes this as his cue to leave, bowing obsequiously once again, 'Yes, my liege'.

But as he steps back, Dr King instead steps even closer, looking VanWest straight in the eyes, 'One last thing... This frizzy-haired thing, this demon that haunts your mind. Lest you know not better, kill it if it comes close. Do not hesitate! It is evil! Do you listen'?

'Yes, my liege'.

The Colonel approaches, he bows too but not so obsequiously, announcing, 'My liege, departure to Earth has commenced, everything has been arranged'.

'Good, everyone be gone'! Dr King replies, with a dismissive wave of his hand, turning back to study his holomap.

As VanWest leaves towards the corridor, the spaceship thrusts upwards, to begin its journey to Earth.

Commissioner Ming stops VanWest, his breath warm and rancid at the door, 'Captain VanWest be sure to hydrate and rest well. Quarters are on C deck'.

Collecting a jelly-like capsule of water at the HyperCreator, VanWest salutes the Commissioner as well as the Colonel and with a sigh of relief steps into the elevator. His mind continues to race, barely able to comprehend all he has witnessed and been told today, including meeting the leader of the Universal Council. If that wasn't enough, he has learnt that time-travel actually exists, and what's more, this evil cult known as the Utopians has it!

VanWest peers out through the transparent module as the elevator zooms to C deck. In-between the darkness, he can see planet Earth. Its incarnadine sea encircles desert-like and naples-yellow landmasses. In places the land is more of a faint dull grey, marking areas where once great cities stood, now parched and abandoned. Earth in 3000 bears little resemblance to itself a millennia ago. Indeed, it now mirrors its sister planet Venus, its surface also obscured by thick, acidic clouds.

The elevator comes to a halt opposite a large rectangular pod. As he enters, a voice from its command recognition system greets him, offering a range of amenities to use: a shower, toilet, bed, kitchen, study, and a simulator. Collectively known as a Hypersphere pod, it is designed to aid in long-distance space travel and exploration; to be a useful remedy for space dementia and fatigue. This machine is much more elaborate than any VanWest has used before and contains over a hundred programs, including a tropical jungle, sandy beaches, hot springs, the red mountains of Mars, and visions of the Milky Way galaxy.

Overwhelmed, he elects only for sleep. The Hypersphere responds by running a program that lulls him into a dream state as he leans back against the padded wall. Closing his eyes, he finds himself back in the conference room lined with rows of white-clothed tables. This time there is a woman, not the frizzy-haired woman as in his other visions; instead, a petite blonde woman wearing a Russian Cossack ski hat. As he walks over, she moves further back, edging ever closer to a podium at the far side of the room.

As he tries to reach out to her, a ringing noise penetrates the room as the scene begins to fade. He finds himself standing upright outside his pod, his Moggle X lenses active and flashing *04:58:00*. Indicating that it's time to commence training for his time travel mission to 1951 Paris!

Staring at his reflection in the elevator's mirrors, he's no longer dressed in a medical gown but his standard-issue off-world Enforcer patrol uniform: a blue skin-tight radioactive hazmat suit with a mask covering his nose and mouth, an indication that he's going to a less habitable zone on Earth. All of his bionic upgrades, taken out in Ward B, have been returned.

The elevator reaches the transporter at the spaceship's entrance, where a bolt of green light sends him onto the naples-yellow sand he saw from space. It's a place he has never travelled to before, lying in the distance he can see a settlement from yesteryear now in ruin. Once-mighty high-rise skyscrapers still dominate its skyline, hollowed out, many partially enveloped in sand dunes.

In front of him is a rusty signpost. Badly corroded, its faint letters read *Welcome to the Province of New Jersey*, with smaller letters underneath, *Liberty and Prosperity 1776*.

Chapter 5   Time Travel Training

A dust storm sweeps towards him along the desert floor, its form changing slowly as it approaches, transforming into that of a vehicle, a hovertruck with dark tinted windows. It swerves around him before grinding to a halt, sending a blanket of sand over his head. The hovertruck's door slides open to reveal a rather dishevelled looking Colonel Cornelius inside, 'Captain. Get in'!

He sits slouched on his seat with his peaked cap lying on the floor. Quite out of the ordinary for a man known for his strict and tidy appearance in front of his Enforcer trainees. Yet more surprisingly for VanWest is what the Colonel holds, a cigar! Smoking is not only banned, well at least in most places, but carries the penalty of 20 years hard labour, a de facto death sentence for most. The Universal Council view this habit as an egregious and a rebelliousness act of delinquents and deviants.

It's perhaps telling of where they have arrived. They are in New Jersey, and there's a whole other set of rules out here. In this place, it is rumoured that nearly anything is allowed! Well, for 'the Elites'.

'Colonel, greetings... I must ask, why New Jersey? I thought this was a no-go zone for Enforcers', VanWest inquires, saluting him as he takes a seat, deciding it best to not remark on the cigar.

'You'll see soon enough - no Jerseyans venture this far from their subway, PATH'. The Colonel adds with a half-smile, 'They don't like the open air'.

'Colonel, with respect, are you sure'? VanWest estimates that they are only a few miles south of the skyscrapers.

The Colonel puffs his cigar, not one for explaining things, 'Captain, I told you, don't worry about it. No ugly assed mutant will be our bane today'.

VanWest is intrigued for he has never seen a Jerseyan up close. All he has seen are their long thin cargo ships that frequently travel in and out of Earth's orbit. These 'Mutants' have a genetic quirk that causes their skin to look disfigured and deformed. Fish-like gills allow them to breathe and filter the toxic air through their neck; a quirk that has helped them to survive in this inhospitable world. Living deep underground, they have kept their autonomy, in part, through their trading of Papini across the solar system. A revered and useful super drug made from a sweet flavoured mushroom that only grows in the dimly lit and damp passageways of New Jersey's old subway system, the PATH network.

This super drug gives all a unique resistance to the radioactive substances found on Earth and, more crucially, those found in space - making it a must-have for those living and working in the solar system's colonies. The origins of these Jerseyan mutants date back to 25th-century Earth, maybe earlier, when many humans left to the Antarctic or space colonies. They instead chose to take refuge underground, including in this PATH network that connects New York to New Jersey.

A no-go zone for Enforcers. Rumour has it that Elites regularly frequent this place not only to buy Papini but also to indulge in hedonistic passions that are banned in Antarctica, including smoking cigars! The Jerseyans neutrality and anonymity is guaranteed under the PATH agreement, which forbids Universal Council forces from entering without their express permission.

'Colonel, may I ask, what's happening today'? VanWest inquires.

The Colonel unfolds an old school Moggleapp tablet and hands it to him, adding, 'Don't take too long'.

Letters project out onto the seat in front and come together to write *Quantum Training*. As the hovertruck turns around, it reassumes its camouflage form of a desert dust storm and heads towards a sand mound in the distance.

VanWest scrolls through the following instructions:

Time Travel Guide
Nutrition
Ensure that diet is high in fibre, protein and vitamins before departure.
Recommended supplements sources: Insects such as cockroaches; high in protein and minerals including Iron, Zinc and Calcium.
More Information

Sleep
8 hours of sleep before departure.
Position yourself laying on your stomach to reduce blood pressure and stretch before entering bed to reduce the chance of cramps.
More Information

Exercise
Intensive daily training routine to get the body prepared for highly strenuous movements and g-forces when travelling.
More Information

Training Simulations
Step 1 Master the flux:
Learning how to withstand and navigate in extreme environments and pressure.
Attend practical session
Step 2 Mind Control, using the Quantum Communicator:
Focusing the mind to transmit messages through time.
Attend practical session
Step 3 Travelling through time, using the Quantum Accelerator:
How to operate the accelerator and use one's mind to see to the correct location and time.
Attend practical session

The sand mound shifts as the hovertruck comes closer and enters. There's a brightly lit space inside, encircled with tall and wide mirrors, transforming as they step out and commencing a simulation. A deep pool of blue water appears surrounded by rocks with a sign that reads *Forbidden, Flooded Shaft*.

The Colonel hands him a packet of liquid breathing pills called O2Breather. These pills enrich the blood with Oxygen, lowering one's blood pressure and allowing the user to withstand higher pressures found deep under the water. There's a uniform change, the Colonel hands him an aquasuit. This must be the first of today's training simulations, *Step 1 Master the Flux*. A gauge lists the water's depth at one and a half miles deep and a reading of 150 atmospheres.

'Captain, this is the first of your assigned training. Work hard to complete these important steps. You need this to complete your leap to 1951 Paris'.

'Yes, of course, Colonel'.

Trying to be as clear as possible, he instructs, 'Step 1, swim down and collect two concrete blocks at the bottom, bring each one up. Your time is 00:20:00, commencing once you enter the water. Affirmative'?

'Yes, Colonel. Affirmative'!

VanWest approaches the water with caution. After inspecting it for dangers, he takes a deep breath and dives in. The water is icy cold and the torrents beneath quite strong. Swimming deeper, he works hard to avoid being spun around as he heads for the concrete blocks below, reaching the largest block first. Grabbing hold of its handlebar, he pulls forcefully until it shifts and then kicks as hard as possible to return to the surface. The O2Breather pills prove critical to his successful completion.

As soon as he returns to the surface, lifting the first block out of the water, the Colonel instructs him to go back down to collect the second. The second journey is even harder, the pressure has increased. Swimming back up, the weight of the block feels like it has doubled. Despite this, he manages to reach the surface, relieved to exit the icy water.

There is no time to recuperate as *Step 2* commences, *Mind Control, using the Quantum Communicator.*

The Colonel gives new instructions, 'Captain, your next task is to practice sending messages with this Quantum Communicator. Dive back down and use only your thoughts to transmit. Insert the Communicator into one of your nodes behind your ears'.

VanWest, not relishing the thought of diving again in the icy water, does as instructed. The Colonel continues, 'It's now zero seven hundred, you have 1-hour to practice this exercise. Captain, remember to concentrate HARD otherwise the Quantum Communicator will not transmit, Roger that'!

'Yes, Colonel. Affirmative'!

Once more, VanWest dives to the bottom of the shaft, reaching its lowest point where he receives a new message, *Testing, Testing, 1-2-3, Testing, Copy That.*

Distracted by the icy water, he tries his hardest to engage the Quantum Communicator by connecting his brain waves digitally to the device in order to return the simple message 'Roger that'. He can't. Again, and again, word by word, 'Roger... that...' Still, nothing transmits. The 1-hour timeframe quickly ticking down, his breathing becoming more difficult.

The high pressure and cold must be stifling his thinking, disrupting his signal. Surmising that he is thinking in the wrong way, he attempts a more visual approach. Instead of concentrating on transmitting by thinking of each word, he pictures each in his mind. Success! A simple message finally transmits, '*Roger that*'.

Encouraged, he sends a longer sentence, imagining the Colonel's face as he does so, '*Roger that Colonel, One And a Half Miles Under Water, Copy That*'?

Relieved to have succeeded, the training bringing back memories of his tough graduation exams at the Enforcer academy - ones he had hoped not to revisit. He practices some more exchanges with the Colonel before heading back up to the surface.

Upon returning, the simulation disperses, and his aquasuit dries out instantly. He finds himself in an empty white room opposite Dr King. His liege holds a chrome briefcase. This must be

Step 3, *Travelling through time using the Quantum Accelerator*. Dr King beckons VanWest to step forward as he unlocks and opens the case. Inside is a small silver rod-shaped device.

'Behold VanWest'! Dr King exclaims as he takes hold of the rod and squeezes it tightly with his right hand.

As he does so, the rod changes shape and slowly widens. When Dr King removes his hand, the rod remains suspended in mid-air. VanWest can feel its pull, his skin tingling and prickling. The rod continues to widen, a black hole growing in its centre. He gazes forth into the hole as a cold icy wind gushes out and whistles across his face. The black hole, now the size of a man, causes the room to shake and pulls even harder to bring him towards its centre.

'My liege'?

'The Quantum Accelerator, my boy'! Dr King answers.

'It's amazing, so peaceful, but so cold, so very cold', VanWest replies, mesmerised.

'Lest I must ask, you are already familiar with the Quantum Communicator'?

The Colonel replies for VanWest, 'Yes, he is my liege'.

Dr King continues, 'Listen well! Together these two devices allow one to travel to any point in time and communicate between the past and the present'.

VanWest stares at the hole, his mind lost. Dr King tries to explain how it works, 'Using this rod, we can track particles through time, as they join and split, all the way to their origin. The Quantum Accelerator splits these atoms and causes a rift in the time continuum, a temporary portal allowing one to travel back and forth, but only once every 48-hours. It needs this to re-stabilise'!

The portal starts to shut and lose its pull, 'Now this is key... By memorising a photo or painting of a particular time, you can travel to that exact location and time. Are you following'?

VanWest nods, 'Yes, my liege'. At least he's trying his best to but is overwhelmed by all this information. He feels like he is still stuck in a dream, expecting to wake at any moment.

Dr King deactivates the Quantum Accelerator rod, explaining this 'evil' Utopian mission in more detail, 'Lest I say before, there are two. The weak-minded Mad Newton has its prototype and is now bent on targeting the scientists who helped him invent time travel - those who figured out how to split atomic particles. We must stop his mission and retrieve his prototype. This mission, this meeting you foresaw, they are related. Do you follow'?

VanWest replies, doing his best to hide his bewilderment, 'Yes, my liege'.

'Very good. As I explained, you must imagine a place and time to arrive. Otherwise, you may be lost in time like the countless chimps it was tested on'.

VanWest gulps, repeating once again, 'Yes, my liege'.

Dr King signals to the Colonel to hands VanWest his Moggleapp tablet. The Colonel instructs, 'Captain, your training will have to do. We hoped for more time but there is no more. You must leave now'!

VanWest gasps, 'Colonel... now'!?

The tablet automatically syncs and uploads the information to his neurological network. It gives a few more details than the Universal Council's Wiki files:

History
At the end of the Second World War, a handful of visionary scientists imagined creating a European atomic physics laboratory. One that would not only unite European scientists but also allow them to share the increasing costs of nuclear physics facilities. At an intergovernmental meeting of UNESCO in Paris, December 1951, the first resolution on the establishment of a European Council for Nuclear Research was adopted. Two months later, European countries signed an agreement establishing the provisional Council - its acronym CERN was born. At the Council's third session in October 1952, Geneva was chosen as the site of this Laboratory.

Key figures include Chairman Francois de Rose [Image], Swiss Delegate Albert Picot [Image] and Swiss Physicist Paul Scherrer [Image].
UNESCO an acronym for United Nations Educational, Scientific and Cultural Organisation.

UNESCO Meetings. Birth of CERN and Achievements
Several important achievements in particle physics have been made during experiments at CERN: Particle Accelerators, Computer Science and World Wide Web, Large Hadron Collider ...
The CERN Convention was established in July 1953, and in September 1954, the European Organisation for Nuclear Research officially came into being. CERN is a French abbreviation for the European Council for Nuclear Research.

Upon completion of the upload, the Colonel switches to an image of a *SNCASE* branded passenger plane tagged *Paris - Le Bourget Aeroport, 10th of December 1951.*

Dr King explains, 'Our intelligence has indicated a successful jump occurred moments ago to 1951 Paris, 10th of December. The target is this UNESCO meeting where the first resolution leading to the formation of CERN is made. These crazed Utopians believe that this meeting instigated scientific collaboration and advancements of the likes never seen before - eventually destroying the world'.

He steps closer, 'My boy, lest I need to say it again, you MUST visualise this exact image and date. Look at it intensely for a few moments. This is your destination. Focus'!

After waiting, and satisfied VanWest has looked long enough, he continues, 'I caution you that you may encounter the Most Wanted'.

The upload of the Ten NEA fugitives commences, mostly Utopians:

Most Wanted
Pretoria Vonn [Image]
Head of NEA in Capital. Expert in Guerrilla Warfare
Dr Isaac VonHelmann 'Mad Newton' [Image]
NEA. Leader of Utopian Sect, Technology Genius and Universal Council Defector
Jaaro Niemen 'The Finn' [Image]
NEA, Utopian Preacher, Assassin and Explosives Expert
Elektra Del Rey 'Electric Girl' [Image]
NEA, Expert in Guerrilla Warfare, Unconfirmed Utopian Preacher
Ling Ling 'The Seductress' [Image]
NEA. Utopian, Highly skilled at Espionage and Explosives
Lexi LuLu 'The High Priestess' [Image]
NEA. Chief of Utopian Dogma, Utopian Preacher
Cisco Lee 'The Inquisitor' [Image]
NEA. Utopian Preacher, Expert Intelligence Analyst
Charlie LeSouris 'The Hacker' [Image]
NEA. Utopian. Hacking Expert
Houston Lowdanski 'Star Fighter' [Image]
NEA. Second in Command, Top Space Pilot and Smuggler
Ankit Barghav 'The Priest' [Image]
NEA. Utopian Preacher, Sect Spokesman and Media Expert

'These deviants will be in disguise; using facial and genome manipulation to subvert and elude the Universal'.

A final upload commences, *UNESCO Investor Profile 1*, that of his own pseudo-identity, along with instructions on how he is expected to behave and act. The profile contains an *Encyclopaedia of Physics of 1950, French Language (extinct in 2631), Visitor Character Map and Biography of Philanthropist*.

This philanthropist, his pseudo-identity, is *Monsieur Frederic Jacques, born in Brussels, Belgium, 23rd of July 1921*. The Colonel takes back his Moggleapp tablet and hands VanWest a box full of funny-looking items including pieces of paper, a passport and

UNESCO conference ticket. VanWest has never physically touched anything made of paper before, only ever seen it behind panels in displays.

The box also contains what must be items of the 1950s, his upload gives details: a German Luger pistol, black-framed glasses, a gold pocket watch with an empty compartment, and some clothing items - a dark grey suit, waistcoat and pair of gloves. And finally, a purse containing 90,000 French Francs in strangely rectangular-shaped pieces of paper and round metallic coins.

After changing into the grey three-piece suit, he puts the items carefully into the pockets, including the identity papers and money. He straps the Luger pistol to the inside of his leg under his trousers.

The Colonel's final instruction, 'Remember to keep the O2Breather pills with you at all times, you never know when you may need it'. VanWest obliges and fits the pills inside his watch compartment.

'Time is of the essence, ready yourself'! Dr King squeezes the Quantum Accelerator rod, re-activating it once more.

VanWest stares forth numbly; he feels neither excited nor frightened, contemplating what could await him on the other side, the plane and Paris, this City of Light, in 1951. Tentatively, he stretches out his hand, moving his fingertips into the portal. He feels a sensation, like that of freezing cold water. It pulls forcefully, his amber stone pendant lifts up and is sucked inside, his head follows.

The sound of water spiralling around sends him into a trance, his eyes widen, mesmerised by the spectrums of light. The medium then pulls his whole body inside, sending him into an ever-faster spin, as if he were stuck inside a whirlpool. The vortex's colourful light cascading around, he twists and turns for what seems an eternity. Spinning until the light begins to fade, suddenly jolting him forward and ejecting him out.

Chapter 6   Leap to the City of Light

VanWest hurtles headfirst into a pile of luggage. His head woozy, he attempts to sit-up but cannot. He gags instead, the dizzying spin of the vortex has left him wanting to throw up. Trying to use his Quantum Communicator to contact Dr King and Colonel Cornelius he finds himself unable to focus, let alone think graphically of the words he must transmit. Noticing the cold air blowing through, the luggage around him, he realises he must be on the plane that the Colonel showed him! Whilst in flight!

Trying to sit up again, he notices a nametag, *F. de Rose*. It's all very real; he has indeed travelled back in time. This nametag is none other than Francois de Rose, a match to his upload, the Chairman of this important UNESCO meeting that will lead to the formation of CERN.

His mind turns to panic, his first thought is how he can return to the present, he scours through the luggage to find the silver Quantum Accelerator rod. After what feels like too long, he finally locates it, lying on some bags beside a metal vent. Lifting the vent up, he sees there is a small white room above. From, which an awful smell of human excrement emerges! He can only assume this must be the toilet. Even so, he isn't keen to stay in this freezing luggage hold and squeezes through the small opening.

Entering inside the toilet cubicle, he gasps, 'Whoa'!

There is a bizarrely dressed man staring back at him. His reflection in the mirror shows him in his disguise, he can barely recognise himself in his 1950s three-piece suit. A voice startles him, an announcement in French, 'Mesdames et messieurs, votre attention s'il vous plait. Nous atterrirons bientôt'. His bionic implants automatically translates it, notifying him that the plane is about to land.

Being cautious, he opens the door only slightly and peers into a smoky hallway, recognising instantly one of the people seated from his new Wiki files as Francois de Rose. Further confirming that he has indeed gone back in time. Francois looks just like his image, his eyes large and blue, hidden behind thick black-framed glasses. The aisle is also cloudy, smoke rises from ashtrays on nearly every seat. VanWest cannot help but be bemused at the sight of people smoking and drinking lots of wine with bottles and glasses everywhere. Smoking and drinking are hedonistic and forbidden vices, long banned in the year 3000.

A blonde woman in a tight blue uniform and pillbox hat walks up the hallway, inspecting and fastening seatbelts in preparation for the plane to land. Seeing that the woman is turning around, he shuts the door and sits down on the closed toilet seat to wait for the plane's descent. He can feel the plane dropping in altitude, very much puzzled by such a shaky and strange form of landing, he presses his palms against the walls to brace himself. The glass bottles clink and rattle as the plane finally thumps down on the ground, braking - *screech,* and coming to a stop after several long seconds.

The pilot announces their arrival, 'Mesdames et messieurs, bienvenue à Paris - Le Bourget. Descendez-vous, s'il vous plaît'. VanWest switches to 20th-century French vocal integration using his *UNESCO Investor Profile 1.*

VanWest waits for the passengers to disembark, inconspicuously blending in with them as they head for a waiting bus on the tarmac. Walking down the airstair, he is taken aback by the beauty of the blue skies and cannot help but take a moment to enjoy the view. He inhales several deep breaths of the fresh and crisp air, his lungs tingling with pleasure. VanWest can feel his mind and body instantly revitalised. Rarely has he tasted such sweetness before, so pure and unfiltered.

He recomposes himself and follows Francois de Rose onto the bus, which drives on to passport control. There he must join a short queue, taking out his passport he reads it several times to ensure that he is ready to recall any detail.

'Have you not travelled before'?

'Sorry'?

'Your passport has no stamps'? The airport officer quizzes him.

VanWest is forced to improvise, returning a nervous-looking smile, 'Ah, this is a new passport, I lost my old one on my last trip'.

Luckily, it works, 'Oh, I see. I thought it strange. Carry on, Sir, next please'.

Francois has already exited the terminal and steps into a waiting taxi. VanWest hones in, with his bionic implants he is able to listen into Francois's conversation with the taxi driver, 'Hotel Majestic, please'.

Hotel Majestic copies with that of his upload: *the temporary home of UNESCO's preparatory commission when it moved from London to Paris in 1946*. He jumps in the next waiting taxi, a white Renault Frégate car that is typical of this time, and instructs the driver to go to the same place, the hotel situated on 'Avenue Kléber, Hotel Majestic'.

'Of course, welcome to the city of light'! The taxi driver welcomes him.

Worried that the Utopians could strike at any time, he is mindful that he mustn't let Francois out of his sight for too long. His upload describes the chairman as a key figure who plays a pivotal role in the development of the CERN over the next few years. VanWest surmises that this makes him a prime target for those on the *Most Wanted* list. He again attempts to reactivate his Quantum Communicator to update his position. However, his focus is still too poor to transmit a message. These sights around him are so alien, his mind and senses overloaded.

The taxi takes him on an hour-long trip through Paris's cobbled streets, past vibrant marketplaces, green parks and old stone chateaus. For VanWest, this alien scene contrasts starkly against that of the year 3000, he is most surprised to see people walk freely along the sidewalks. Free of harassment from patrol androids and Quadrotors, a big-brother type circular hovercraft that stalks and monitors Antarctica's citizens. Their clothes are straight out of a museum, made of cotton and wool. Their vehicles are four-wheeled cars that disperse foul-smelling black fumes from their exhausts. Nearly everyone smokes, rolling and lighting pieces of white paper, cigarettes, as they walk along the streets.

Even though 1951 Paris bears the scars of World War II, its buildings blackened and dilapidated, it still looks so much cleaner and happier than any settlement he has seen before. Despite there being no leaves on the trees, being December and late Autumn, it's the first time he sees trees of this size in real life. Their trunks so thick and branches spread over the streets. There is life all around.

The taxi driver switches on the radio on the car's dashboard, it plays music. The sound is fuzzy, at times dipping in and out as it loses connection. The radio is so primitive, only having an amplitude-modulated 'AM' frequency range. He recognises one of the tunes from his ColaBeers tour, it is Edith Piaf's *La Vie en Rose*. The song is banned by the Universal Council, its playing a show of defiance by its citizens that risks imprisonment and hard labour if caught.

The only media permitted and broadcasted in the year 3000 is an Elite run channel featuring a small selection of programs: 'the 'Universal Commandment Recitals for Kids', special events such as 'the Universal Games' and every Sunday 'Judgment Day' also known as the 'Day of Executions'.

Despite the seriousness of his mission, it makes all for quite a glamourous and enjoyable ride. He has only ever seen a modified version of Paris via the Hypersphere and, as the old adage goes, there's nothing like the real thing.

A signpost indicates the taxi is approaching *Notre-Dame, arrondissement 4*. He sits up at the sight of a colossal monument, one he has only ever seen in a Hypersphere simulation. Structured in the shape of an archway is the Napoleonic war memorial 'L'Arc de Triomphe', its design Romanesque and neoclassical. He marvels at the arch adorned with commemorative inscriptions and carvings though its stones are blackened by pollution.

The Arc stands in front of the Tour Eiffel. An even larger monument, it still exists in the year 3000 as a corroded relic. Constructed all the way back in 1889, it has long since become a ruin and a distant reminder of a forgotten time. The Tour Eiffel's iron lattice structure reaches an impressive 320 metres tall, in 1951 one of the tallest buildings in the world, close to the length of an SCC class spaceship. La Seine's brownish-blue water meanders alongside these monuments. He has never seen water that was not incarnadine. The whole scene is very surreal.

The taxi turns right on to *Rue La Perouse* towards Hotel Majestic, situated in le Champs-Élysées. At the traffic lights, a young man with an oversized cap comes over from a kiosk and knocks on his window waving a magazine, *Le Courrier*. It's an educational journal, its headline *Les Droits De L'Homme*, translates as 'The Rights of Man'. Thinking it could be useful, he cautiously rolls down his window, taking a few moments to figure out how, and gives the smiling young man a 20 Francs sheet of paper from his money purse.

He flicks through the journal. Although the general UNESCO meeting is mentioned, there's little about the talks on the formation of the European Organisation of Nuclear Research, the creation of CERN itself, and who will be there. Offering him no further clues as to who or what the Utopians could be targeting, no more than he knows already.

The taxi driver indicates that they have arrived at *Hotel Majestic*, pointing at a Beaux-Arts 19th-century style hotel that is several stories high. It has a symmetrical stone facade lavishly decorated with swags, medallions, flowers, and shields. The building exudes wealth and money, a place worthy of hosting Europe's top diplomats, scientists and delegates. As the taxi stops at the entrance, a porter in a red uniform walks over to open his door.

'100 Francs', the taxi driver asks with a big smile.

VanWest hands a piece of paper with the number over to the man and steps out. Seeing that he has no luggage, the porter directs him through the front door to *La Réception*.

The man's piercing blue eyes look strangely familiar. However, VanWest is distracted by the marvellous building in front. Walking into the hotel's grand foyer, which is adorned with bright white flowers and hanging crystal chandeliers, it somewhat reminds him of the *Universalis Domum de Praeterito*, the rococo chamber he entered upon winning the Games. Here, Renaissance art decorates the walls, and statues of illustrious French nobles and scientists line its hallways.

He spots Francois de Rose at the reception and watches him from a distance to see what room key he receives. Following, he asks the clerk for a room close by, pretending that he is a colleague, 'Same floor as Francois, please'.

Francois does not go directly to his room. Instead, he stops at the bar for a drink and cigarette.

Even though there are no visible dangers in the foyer or the stairway, VanWest conducts a sweep of the area to check for any sign of the *Most Wanted*. Using his bionic implants, he runs an image recognition scan against the humans loitering, returning 'Nothing Out Of Place'.

Several middle-aged men are lounging in the bar area drinking glasses of wine, as on the plane. Their accents identify them to be Swiss, each talks keenly about the advantages of collaboration and their thoughts on the formation of a nuclear agency. VanWest wants to know more, but he suddenly finds himself distracted by a petite lady with long blonde hair and big brown eyes, sitting on a barstool. She wears a shiny silver necklace that rests on her perky bosom, pushed up by her skimpy black cocktail dress. He's never seen a woman dressed this way, so alluringly, not in a loosely fitted jumpsuit.

Her brown eyes cross his, and she gives him a smile, biting her lower lip slightly, before turning to greet the man next to her, whom VanWest recognises from his upload as *Albert Picot*; a Swiss delegate and a key figure in successfully lobbying for the CERN site to be built in Geneva, Switzerland.

Francois leans on the bar's counter, giving VanWest a wink, he orders two glasses of wine, 'My friend, a lady of the night, be careful... They are not normally permitted in such fine places'.

Francois hands VanWest a glass of wine. He has never had a drink before. VanWest smiles and, for the sake of the mission, tepidly takes a few sips, his *Investor Profile* indicating it as a requirement for blending in. The taste is strange, dry and fruity, but makes him instantly slightly light-headed.

Francois smiles, 'What's your name, here for the conference'?

'Van... I mean Frederic Jacques, and yes'! VanWest replies, nearly forgetting his pseudo-identity.

'Well, Frederic, my friend, be careful. Have yourself a splendid evening', Francois winks, picking up his drink and walking away to join a table with several other UNESCO members.

Still quite disorientated from his leap and travel through time, the drink does not help his concentration. VanWest glances over at the lady, hesitating for a second as he decides to take Francois's advice to stay clear. He puts his glass down and leaves to get some rest, his room key in his hand. There doesn't seem to be any danger here.

Making his way up the stairs, his Quantum Communicator finally activates, and a short-scrambled message transmits through. It is from Dr King, *'Beware, They Are In Disguise, Beware The Assassin Jaaro'*. Unnervingly, just as he finishes receiving the message, there is a loud creaking noise. Reaching his floor, he finds the porter that welcomed him into the hotel. He doesn't have the same face as the assassin *Jaaro the Finn* but looking at the *Most Wanted* images he does have the same piercing blue eyes.

The porter very slowly pushes a trolley filled with plates and glasses through the hallway. VanWest's hands begin to tremble, his instinctive tick that he has come to know forewarns of trouble ahead. The porter looks over at him, placing his hand over a silver serving plate with a roller lid as he creeps closer. VanWest sees his room is located one door away, walking in quickstep, he unlocks the door and hurries inside, slamming it shut behind him.

Diving behind the bed, he can hear the porter's trolley approaching - *clink*. Two knocks on the door follow before the porter calls to him by his pseudo name, 'Monsieur Jacques, a special welcome platter. Compliments of Hotel Majestic'.

VanWest puts his hand in his trousers, pulling out the Luger pistol strapped against his leg, and presses his index finger against its trigger, readying to draw. But as the door unlocks and slowly opens, the porter's head peers around with a big smile. VanWest quickly places a pillow over the pistol. The porter does not appear to have noticed it. The serving plate lid is now fully open and contains only fruit.

After placing it down on the table, the porter exits with a friendly nod, 'Have a good evening'.

VanWest keeps his finger on his pistol's trigger and, after waiting a few moments, decides to follow him with the pillow still over it, remaining suspicious that this is Jaaro the Finn. Stepping into the corridor, the lights have dimmed. He looks right and left down the hallway, the porter nowhere to be seen, seemingly having disappeared with only his trolley remaining.

Creak! A noise coming from the stairwell causes him to turn sharply, ready to shoot.

It's not the porter but Francois. His cheeks a rosy red, he walks past VanWest, 'Goodnight, my friend', and enters the room next to his.

VanWest waits for Francois to close his door before returning to his own room, wondering if this porter was indeed Jaaro and if so will he return. Everything calmer, he has time to survey his room. It is quite strange, void of electronics except for a tube radio on a wooden cupboard. There is no holoscreen, no recharging pod, just a large bed covered with a green bedspread. Beside it, floor-length drapes made from the same cloth cover the window.

Too agitated and worried to sleep, he decides to stand guard for the next few hours, checking the hallway and surveying the street from his balcony. The effects of time travel start to catch up. Scanning the fruit left by the porter, it returns that it is safe to take a bite. Feeling no ill effect, and now very hungry, he eats the rest.

Its taste so very juicy, fresh and sweet, unlike anything he has eaten before.

He also has some time to think through the mission, trying to figure out the Utopian plan he keeps returning to the same question: why are they waiting to strike at the conference and not before? Everyone in the hotel is very much unguarded and an easy target. It doesn't make sense. What exactly are they hoping to achieve?

As the night wears on into the morning, he finally lays down on the edge of his bed. Its mattress springy and comfortable, he is no longer able to stay awake and drifts off. Dreaming of the woman at the bar, this so-called 'lady of the night', her big brown eyes and long blonde hair seductively drooped over her shoulders. Biting her lower lip, she calls him closer.

Chapter 7   The Orchestra

Toot! The loud noise from an automobile horn wakes him. He has slept until mid-afternoon and feels quite drowsy. While asleep, a flyer has been slipped under his room door, advertising the *Paris Orchestra, Salle Pleyel, this evening at 7pm*. He tries to activate his Quantum Communicator, but his focus is still not strong enough to reply to Dr King.

VanWest is annoyed with himself, he should have been watching the hallway. Still wearing his 3-piece suit, he makes his way to the foyer to check on the UNESCO delegates as well as Francois de Rose. To his relief, he finds Francois talking to a man, the Swiss physicist Paul Scherrer.

Eavesdropping, he hears Scherrer passionately making the case that, 'Geneva must be the home of CERN, the Collider has the backing of the state, this must be the central point to any agreement'.

He goes on, 'No other country is neutral enough; no other place more suitable for Europe's elite scientists and their families; no country willing to invest as much capital'.

Francois politely stops the conversation, 'Let's discuss after the recital'.

'That reminds me, I need to go to Les Galeries to try on a black tuxedo for Salle Pleyel. I've been eating too many cakes lately', Scherrer jokes before departing.

Francois, and likely many others attending the conference, will be at the orchestra tonight. Realising this could be a perfect target for the *Most Wanted*, he decides to follow Scherrer and buy a tuxedo as well. At the hotel's entrance, VanWest finds a new porter, the suspicious acting one nowhere to be seen, who flags over a waiting taxi with a small wave and opens the passenger door.

VanWest tells the driver to follow behind Scherrer, 'Follow that car, Les Galeries, please'.

The destination is not too far and the taxi soon comes to a halt outside a department store, *Galeries Lafayette*. The window displays human-like models, strangely stuck in a pose neither moving nor talking. Curious he checks his Wiki, which returns that these are advertising mannequins, dressed to entice passing shoppers into the shop to buy expensive items.

Walking inside, the displays are immaculate, every detail perfect. The food hall has fruit-shaped murals on its walls and ceiling. He takes the escalator to the clothes section, which is filled with hundreds of suits separated by colour and brand. Scherrer is at the shop counter, talking to the clerk about fitting his tuxedo. VanWest discretely walks to his side and asks the other man behind the counter for a similar tuxedo, giving him his precise measurements.

'Very well, Sir! That's 280 Francs, please. You need it for the orchestra? I will send your grey suit to your place, no charge. Where are you staying'?

'Hotel Majestic', VanWest replies, handing the smiling man three pieces of paper with 100 Francs written on it.

Scherrer has since left, and it's already getting dark. VanWest goes outside. Copying the others, he waves his arm to hail a taxi. The taxis with two lights on at the top seem to be the ones accepting passengers. A small beige Renault taxi pulls in, and VanWest instructs the driver to take him to Salle Pleyel orchestra hall, in the 8th arrondissement. Soon VanWest reaches the destination. It looks like one of the palaces that VanWest saw in the Hypersphere. The magnificent orchestra hall, built of white stone with a blue roof, sits prominently on a street lined with decorative displays and green pine trees. Several signs read *Joyeux Noel*.

In front is a scene full of pomp and pageantry. Shiny cars pull in to drop off people in fancy attire: men in black tuxedos alongside glamorously dressed women, each wrapped in a fur coat that partially conceal long strapless dresses. VanWest used to only seeing women in jumpsuits, observes that each dress is slightly different in design and hugs their figures. The women walk coquettishly up a worn red carpet, occasionally stopping to greet someone with a distant kiss on each cheek as they make their way inside the hall.

He checks his Quantum Communicator and, finding no new message, joins the queue to the ticket booth. Studying the floorplan displayed on the wall whilst he waits. He opts for an expensive upper-tier box, hoping it will give him a good view of the audience and the European delegates attending.

After purchasing his ticket, he walks upstairs, passing several white pillars, and enters into an auditorium that stands over 30-foot high. Rows of burgundy red seats face a relatively small semi-circular stage, its shape similar to that of a Greek theatre, crowded with various instruments. Percussion instruments at the back, wind and string at the front, none of, which VanWest has ever seen live. The musicians are also dressed in black tuxedos, seated behind their instruments, they look up at a man who stands authoritatively on a small podium in front, with his back to the audience. This must be the conductor.

Led to his box by an usher, he sits down and leans over the balcony to check for anything suspicious. In the boxes opposite, he quickly locates the European delegates, already seated, helping themselves to glasses of wine and champagne, which the ushers serve freely.

The usher leads a woman into his box, VanWest recognises her instantly, it is the attractive blond lady from the hotel bar. By chance, she has been seated next to him. He cannot help but stare at her as she walks seductively to her seat in her skin-tight long blue dress, which pushes her cleavage together and out, as with her black cocktail dress from earlier. Equally captivating are her sultry brown eyes. She gifts him a quick smile as she bites her lower lip before taking her seat. Her sweet scent making him slightly dizzy.

The conductor holds a black baton half-raised in his right hand, waiting for the audience to quieten down - *hush*. In the year 3000, the only remaining philharmonic is exclusively for the entertainment of the Elites. He feels oddly privileged, very few ever get to witness such a sight and hear live music from such instruments. VanWest forces himself to temper his enthusiasm and remain focused. His mission is to guard the delegates and stay alert for signs of the *Most Wanted*, in particular, the man he believes to be Jaaro The Finn.

The composer wields his baton, the auditorium now completely silent, to begin his rendition of *Symphonie fantastique: Épisode de la vie d'un Artiste...en cinq parties*. The programme lists five movements:

1. Rêveries - Passions (Daydreams - Passions)
2. Un bal (A ball)
3. Scène aux champs (Scene in the Country)
4. Marche au supplice (March to the Scaffold)
5. Songe d'une nuit de sabbat (Dream of a Witches' Sabbath)

VanWest can't help but be moved by the music, each note stirring his emotions. He imagines the scenery and setting behind each. Each so different, each with its own unique story. The music also brings back sad memories, tears start to well up as it casts him back to the burning slums in ColaBeers. The screams of innocent citizens caught in the destruction, of women incinerated whilst shielding their children. The NEA rebel leader being tortured to death. He struggles to comprehend how any of this could be justified.

The captivating woman spots his tears and with a smile offers him her white handkerchief. Their eyes lock, transfixed on one another for a moment.

'I adore a man with emotion', she whispers in a velvety voice.

'Thank you', VanWest replies, slightly embarrassed.

Glancing at the UNESCO delegation on the balcony opposite, she says, 'I admire a man like you that can follow the music and its tales. Those hedonistic creatures over there I bet cannot... Look at them, lining their guts with wine and champagne, can you imagine how they live'.

VanWest is bemused by her comments, acting as if she is an observer like him, not quite at ease with this scene and from this time. Before he can reply, he notices that his hands are trembling. Looking back at this balcony, the pretty lady has alerted him to a potential danger as one of the ushers looks a lot like the hotel porter, Jaaro. If so, he's very close to the UNESCO delegates. Panicked, he excuses himself. Forgetting to return the handkerchief, he hurries out into the semi-circular corridor behind, quickly pulling out and cocking his Luger pistol.

As he runs to the other side of the orchestra, unbeknownst to him the porter come usher has noticed him too. Now hidden behind a pillar, he lies in wait armed with a cutting wire. The usher leaps out as VanWest passes, attempting to wrap the wire around his neck.

As a well-trained Enforcer, VanWest reacts instinctively by blocking the wire with his pistol and forcing the usher backwards, slamming him against the wall, knocking - *crash* - a glass vase, filled with long-stemmed roses, to the floor. The fifth act commences as he struggles to break free, with only the pistol keeping the wire from slicing his neck open.

'Monsieur Jacques, or should I say Captain VanWest... don't make this more painful than this needs to be', he taunts.

VanWest hooks his right leg behind Jaaro's, throwing them both to the floor. With the wire still pressed against his pistol, he manages to grab hold of a shard from the broken vase, and despite it cutting into his hand, he stabs it into the usher's shoulder, releasing himself. VanWest does not hesitate, he rolls over and fires a volley into Jaaro's chest. The shots fire in rhythm and tempo of the music muffles the loud bangs as red blood splashes across the wall behind.

Immediately, the usher's body starts to twitch, his face and hands transforming, growing paler and paler, to reveal his true form, of the *Most Wanted, Jaaro The Finn*.

VanWest looks up and down the corridor to check if anyone has seen or heard the commotion and for any more incoming threats. Fortunately, there is no one, all remains quiet. Still, he must leave fast. Mindful not to change the time continuum, he first strips Jaaro of his implants and anything that could identify him. For if he was found with these items, none of, which existed in the mid-20th century, it could change the future. In Jaaro's chest pocket, he finds Mad Newton's prototype Quantum Accelerator rod. It has been dented by one of his bullets and is no longer useable.

His best option is to escape before the alarm is raised and the police arrives. VanWest runs down the stairs to the front of the building, sneaking past a couple of ushers. Pulling in is a black Citroën 11, a vehicle he could use to get away. He waits for the valet to exit the car, and with no one else close by, knocks him out cold with a swift and discrete blow to the side of his head. Careful and precise, so not to cause permanent injury to the valet - just as he was taught by his Enforcer academy professor, Master Jiang.

VanWest jumps into the driver's seat but is slightly stumped by the unfamiliar car controls. He has raced with a shift-stick car in a Hypersphere simulation but the real thing is quite something to behold. With a turn of the key he starts the ignition, causing the car to lunge forward followed by a loud *vroom*. Shifting the gear stick left and forward, he presses his foot on the pedal to accelerate.

The car swerves out into the traffic - *screech!* His erratic driving lets him down as he catches the attention of a police car stationed nearby. The blue police sign at the top of a small black and white Renault 4CV car starts to flash and a siren sounds - *Wah-Wah!* Two officers on the sidewalk race towards him, flagging for him to stop. When he fails to do so, they draw their guns and fire at his tires to try to disable his car - *pop, pop* - one of the bullets ricochets and shatters his windscreen, narrowly missing his head. VanWest spins 180-degrees and manoeuvres down a narrow side street.

Much to VanWest's dismay, the small police car is faster and more manoeuvrable than it looks, it closes in. He floors the gas pedal and turns into a busy street heavy with traffic. Swerving onto a packed sidewalk, he crashes through a series of souvenir kiosks, narrowly missing the shocked pedestrians. Without slowing down, he aims for a bridge not too far away, a crossing over *La Seine*. Unfortunately, because of the conference the area is heavily guarded and several more police cars lie in wait ready to block his path.

Pop! Pop! The waiting police fire at his tires, piercing this time his front driver-side tire and sending his vehicle careening off the road - *bang* - crashing through the black iron and stone railing, down into the river. His head smashes into the steering wheel as the black Citroën 11 splashes into the water, knocking him unconscious. The strong currents quickly dragging the car beneath and filling it with the dirty brown water that flows through his shattered windscreen.

VanWest finds himself no longer in the car, he is instead standing opposite Alpha who holds a laser dagger against the neck of the frizzy-haired woman he saw before. Although her hair partially covers her face, he notices that she looks very much like the woman in Ward B, Nurse Rose. There too is a familiar and cold voice, that of Dr King repeating the same sentence, 'Lest I must say, she is evil'. Ignoring the voice, he calls out to this woman, only to wake gasping.

His body is submerged in icy cold water, which reaches his neck and threatens to drown him; panic sets in as he furiously tries to swim out but the current is too strong, especially for his now weary and cold body. He spots his O2Breather pills, dislodged from his watch's compartment, floating above the dashboard. He stretches out, just able to grab hold of one. Swallowing quickly, the oxygen reinvigorates him and gives him enough energy to force his way out through the shattered windscreen. Swimming against the force of the water, like he did during his time-travel training, he reaches the surface and manages to clamber onto a moored dinghy. The Colonel's training and recommendation of taking these pills have saved his life.

After coughing up the brown water, he lies down for a minute in the dinghy. Exhausted but very much alive, he is relieved to spot the lights of the Eiffel tower. As luck would have it, the current seems to have taken him downstream, away from the police, and close to his hotel. His clothes soaked and his body shivering from the cold, he takes off his jacket and wrings out the river's water.

Fortunately, the darkness allows him to make his way back to the hotel unnoticed. He, nevertheless, keeps his head bowed to conceal his face, sneaking through the lobby and past the reception, careful not to draw attention. He then hurries up the stairs to his floor. Shivering uncontrollably from the cold, his skin is pale, hypothermia is a serious risk if he doesn't warm up fast. He struggles to unlock the door to his room, his hands shaking so much. Once inside, he strips off and runs a hot bath. The hot water returns a tinge of colour as he scrubs his body with a bar of soap, trying to cleanse himself of the river's dirt.

Chapter 8   Beware the Seductress

Soaking in the warm water, VanWest hears a gentle knock on his door. Slipping out of the bathtub, he grabs a towel and wraps it around his waist before tiptoeing to the door. He no longer has his Luger pistol, lost in the river, and after the events at the orchestra is quite wary of what will happen next. To his amazement, he sees through the peephole the captivating blonde woman still dressed in her gorgeous blue dress. Excited and without thinking, he opens the door.

'Hello there', he welcomes her.

'Well, hello there too... I've come for my handkerchief', she asks with a suggestive smile, her sultry eyes locked onto his.

'Oh! My apologies'! VanWest replies in a serious tone, not quite understanding her intent.

She moves closer, 'Why did you leave? A man was shot, and I was so scared it may... be you', she tells him in a concerned tone, now looking lustfully at his muscular upper body, gently stroking it with her fingertips as she steps inside his room.

'Oh, really? That's terrible, I had to leave for an urgent matter. That's shocking to hear', he feigns shock.

After retrieving her now soaked handkerchief, tucked in the trouser pocket of his tuxedo, he turns to find her no longer standing at the door. Instead, she is sitting on his bed half undressed, her long slender legs stretched across, revealing a small green tattoo with the letter *U*. He walks over transfixed by her sultry brown eyes and luscious lips. Sitting down beside her, she strokes her hand up his arm to his neck before locking lips as they kiss, sending his body into a blissful rush.

He arrives in a room filled with rows of desks, packed with hunched over men with clunky looking headphones. The men look familiar, Francois de Rose sits at the front, facing the delegates. He's speaking into a metal microphone, 'assist and encourage the formation of laboratories in order to increase international scientific collaboration'.

As Francois talks, VanWest notices something odd, a woman hiding in the far corner of the room. Her face is partly obscured by her large Russian Cossack Ski hat. He tries to step forward and get a better view, but as he does so - *bang* - he is knocked to the floor. He attempts to stand up but awakens back on his hotel bed, covered from head to toe in sweat.

He looks around for the captivating blond woman but she is gone. Checking the nightstand, in the hope that she might have left a note, he's alarmed to find that all his items are missing: his Quantum Communicator and, most worrying, both Quantum Accelerator rods, including the dented one he took from Jaaro. Furthermore, his identity card with his alias Monsieur Frederic Jacques is gone too and his ticket to the UNESCO meeting. It finally dawns on him that this was no normal woman or ordinary fling, that he has been well and truly duped, another victim of the infamous *Ling Ling 'The Seductress'*. Her photo was even on the *Most Wanted* list.

Even after Dr King's mission briefing, he allowed himself to be tricked, spellbound by her allure and charm. His lust having clouded his common sense. The *U tattoo* was another missed sign, as well as her odd comments about the 'hedonistic' delegates in the orchestra. Smacking his palm against his forehead, he rues his stupidity. He and his mission are in serious jeopardy!

'The Seductress has effectively trapped him in 1951 Paris if he cannot find her before she leaps. With over 48 hours the future will be changed, having past the required time to stabilise the Quantum Accelerator between each leap, she may already have leapt. The noise of revving automobile engines and people shouting draws him to his balcony.

Peering down, he notices that the street is bustling with officials and delegates. Furthermore, he is alarmed to see a large sign directing everyone to the hotel's conference centre. *UNESCO!* He has slept all the way to the morning of the 15th of December. The meeting is today. The Seductress must have drugged him!

Still half-dazed, he walks into the hallway, forgetting he's undressed, and steps on a scrunched-up piece of paper. Opening it up, there is a number written, the number corresponds with the wing accommodating the Swiss delegates. It suddenly dawns on him what exactly is happening. Finally, he links the pieces together: his visions of the woman in the Cossack hat, the drugging, the blast. Today being the UNESCO meeting, it's clear that the Seductress and the Utopians have plotted an event so enormous that its ramifications would be felt far longer than just a year or a decade. It's all starting to make sense.

Barely six years since World War II, Europeans scientists have only begun to work in an organised and collaborative way on new scientific projects. He concludes that the Seductress must be seeking to break the trust between them in the most harmful way possible. The Utopians interpret this creation of CERN as part of the 20th-century philosopher Hans Ashtar's warning that the rapid advancement of technology and machines would bring an end to an Utopian Earth.

VanWest continues to piece together the clues. At both the bar and orchestra, the Seductress was close to the Swiss delegates including Albert Picot and Paul Scherrer. She was also watching Francois de Rose, the Chairman for the meeting and the CERN site's Kingmaker, a key decision-maker on its formation and location. During this time, the Swiss, led by Picot and Sherrer, have been trying to persuade Francois that their country should be the headquarters of this new agency, in Geneva.

Could it be that she is plotting to not only kill Francois but also implicate the Swiss in his murder? It would be very smart indeed. Not only would the location of CERN not be in Switzerland, but it would also sow distrust between already sceptical European nations. And CERN itself would likely not come into formation for decades, if not centuries.

Fortunately, seeing that the delegates, scientists and businessmen are all still arriving, there is time to stop her. She hasn't acted yet! Robbed of his pistol and identity card, he wonders what he can actually do and how he even can enter the conference.

Clatter! A loud noise, like that of plates and cutlery rattling, disrupts his thinking. At the other end is a man in a red uniform pushing a trolley. Whilst rationally he knows this cannot be the assassin Jaaro, his newfound paranoia of hotel staff leads him to retreat into his room and shut the door. After a couple of minutes, the trolley stops outside his room and a knock follows. VanWest cautiously peers through the peephole to get a better look, finding that he carries his grey three-piece suit meticulously folded across his forearm. He reasons this man to be a genuine employee of the hotel. Galleries Lafayette must have returned it this morning. It's good to have his suit but the employee's red uniform gives him a better idea. If he were seen to be hotel staff, he might be able to enter the conference without needing his pseudo-identity card. This uniform might just do the trick! Furthermore, he could use the employee's master key to search the hotel for the Seductress and delegates.

Executing his plan, VanWest opens the door to let the man in and, upon entering, he slams his head against the wall, knocking him out cold, a blow likely to keep him out for the next few hours. Just like with the car valet, he is careful to not cause permanent damage. He strips the employee of his uniform, before laying him on his bed and taking his master key.

He leaves to first check Francois de Rose's room, nothing out of the ordinary. Then follows the number on the paper, which takes him to the wing housing the Swiss delegates. Knocking on the doors, he lets himself into their rooms and conducts a swift biometric sweep of each. Besides the fact that their briefcases are gone, they already have left, he finds nothing out of the ordinary. He sighs, ready to leave for the conference but, being naturally thorough, checks the last remaining room at the end of the hallway, which belongs to Albert Picot.

Whilst the room is clean, a peculiar black powder on the bed catches his attention. Kneeling beside it, he wonders what it is. He checks the bathroom and finds yet more black powder spilt over the floor. It all supports his hypothesis that the Swiss are being implicated in a plot. This powder is some sort of primitive explosive. What's more, it looks like it was left here on purpose, not to kill anyone as its amount is too little, but rather to incriminate Albert Picot. The visions, the powder, the pieces of the puzzle all start to fit into place.

The noise of engines revving and people shouting draws him to the window. Below, the crowd has grown even larger with spectators, photographers and journalists now jostling for position near the hotel's entrance. *Click-click!* Oddly shaped large cameras on tripods flash to take the photos of the delegates and scientists. In the commotion, he spots a grey Russian Cossack ski hat, the same hat as the one in his vision. It's the woman who so skilfully seduced him, the Seductress. She walks to the entrance with a man dressed in a brown suit and waistcoat.

VanWest opens the window and leans over to get a better view, it is Francois de Rose! A *Most Wanted* is walking in with the UNESCO meeting's chairman. This cannot be!? Indeed, it was he who warned to stay away from this 'lady of the night'. Has she cast her spell over him too? VanWest immediately leaps into action, running out his room and down the stairs, hoping to intercept her at the foyer. But he's too late, by the time he arrives, the Seductress is at security and, without any holdup, is allowed through into the conference centre.

Wearing the ill-fitting red uniform, VanWest enacts his audacious plan to enter the conference as a hotel employee. Grabbing hold of a pitcher of water from the side table, he approaches a security guard. The man looks at him with some suspicion, as if not quite believing him to be an employee. However, with a large group of delegates approaching, he opts to wave VanWest on, allowing him into the conference and into a room that looks very familiar. Like déjà vu, it is all becoming a bit too real; the puzzle completing itself and the plot taking shape. However, the Seductress is now nowhere to be seen. He knows he must find her fast.

As VanWest foresaw, hunched-backed delegates sit in front of rows of white-clothed desks, listening intensely into their bulky headphones, as translators speak to them quietly. Francois is seated centre stage, looking relaxed but authoritatively towards the delegates. He greets the room with a big smile, 'Welcome my friends to this UNESCO meeting', and sets about outlining today's agenda in a firm and clear voice.

The agenda includes a session to discuss the pros and cons of an international agreement for the creation of the European Organisation of Nuclear Research, CERN: 'The first resolution'. If this is the place he envisioned, the Seductress will act soon. Trying not to panic, he discreetly walks along each row of white-clothed tables, filling the empty glasses with the water from his pitcher whilst searching for her. Where is she!?

With so many delegates and the meeting's chairman Francois speaking, he worries that an explosion is nigh, for everything is set in place. Continuing to move from row to row, he switches his attention to finding any trace of the black powder from Albert Picot's room, but he cannot find this either. He wonders what is he not seeing?

Leaning his back against the wall, he looks back over at Francois. Like with everywhere in 1951 Paris, smoking is permitted inside this meeting too. This time, he notices something very worrying: tiny black specs on Francois's brown jacket! Could this be the explosive powder!?

Worse yet, he sees that Francois holds a lighter in his left hand. The Seductress's full plot finally unveiled and the puzzle complete. A spark from the lighter could ignite the black powder on his jacket and blow his head right off, with Albert Picot implicated for his murder. VanWest knows he must act straight away. To his right is a fire alarm box, and without hesitation pulls down the lever, keeping one eye firmly fixed on Francois.

Pin-pong! Pin-pong! The alarm sounds before Francois can light his cigarette. His quick thinking may have worked! Francois places his lighter and cigarette down on his desk and calmly instructs through his microphone, 'My friends, we must go'! Before proceeding to the exit.

Still holding a now half-empty pitcher of water, VanWest knows the danger isn't over, the powder is still on Francois's clothes. He intercepts him, pretending to trip, he throws the water all over him, soaking his jacket and shirt and, more importantly, the powder. Remembering only at that moment that Francois has seen his face before, he bows his head, trying to avoid eye contact.

'Apologies, Sir. Me so clumsy', VanWest offers in broken English, trying his best not to raise suspicion.

'Agh! You have done me a favour, my friend! There are black stains all over my jacket. I found it in this dirty state when I passed through security. Strangely, it was clean when I entered the building', Francois responds kindly.

'Thank you. Many apologies', mumbles VanWest, head still bowed.

But, as VanWest helps Francois remove his jacket, the jig is up. Francois makes eye contact with him and asks, 'Do I not know you from somewhere'?

Before he can offer an excuse, VanWest finally catches sight of the woman in the grey Cossack ski hat, the Seductress - she has been watching them from the stairwell, half-hidden by a mahogany grandfather clock. A now very concerned Francois calls 'Security' as VanWest drops the jacket to give chase to the Seductress.

She turns and runs into what seems to be the cellar. Rushing down the stairs, he is forced to duck as he follows. Entering into a pitch-black room with a low ceiling, greeting him is icy cold air that whistles past - *phwwwhht* - so forcefully it causes the wine bottles on the racks to rattle. The wind is most peculiar as there is no window, no visible source from where the cold air could originate. He uses his hands to search from rack to rack to find her, hastened by the approaching shouts of the hotel's security, 'Down there'.

The hairs on his arms are standing straight as if being pulled towards something. Upon reaching the last rack, a wine bottle smashes on the floor. The Seductress leaps out, brushing VanWest's shoulder as she passes. He manages to grab hold of the tail end of her fur coat, thinking he has caught her, but instead finds himself yanked sideways.

The darkness of the cellar is replaced by an intense light. Once again he is spinning around and around uncontrollably through the vortex, just like his journey to 1951 Paris. His arms flail about, trying to grab hold of something, anything!

Finally, it comes to a halt, jolting him out and crashing into a mushy - *splash* - and gooey bed of paste. Dazed, he struggles to sit up and get to his feet. Even though he is not gagging this time, he knows he has travelled through time again! By the layout of the building, dimly lit with metal grids and a floor caked with gooey paste, he must have leapt into a farm.

Managing to get to his feet, a loud *hiss* noise stops him still. He gulps before turning around slowly. A giant creature stares back at him, its small head striped black and red with antennas sticking out, balancing on top of a large elongated body with long spindly legs.

It's a giant farm-bred cockroach. Whilst freaky in appearance, fortunately for VanWest it is ever so timid. He picks up a handful of the gooey paste, likely fodder, and throws it at the bug, causing it to scamper away. However, it only serves to reveal yet more farm-bred cockroaches behind! The Seductress hasn't chosen the most glamourous of locations, especially when compared to 1951 Paris! He wonders, why here?

Farm cockroaches are a popular delicacy on Earth, prized in particular for their high protein and fat contents. Over recent centuries, they have been bred to be far larger and fatter than their much smaller ancestors. Able to withstand the effects of radioactive chemicals, these bugs thrived in the soaring temperatures when most other creatures perished. Splurging on the toxic waste dumps, which contributed to their dramatic increase in size. Although farm cockroaches are relatively tame, several humans over the years have been killed and eaten by their wilder cousins, who live in the sewers.

A small light emanates from the other side of the pen, casting two human shadows before it. The first is the Seductress, he found her! The other a large bulky man, perhaps the cockroach farmer judging by his large metal axe. VanWest decides to creep closer, careful though not to be seen or heard. He doesn't know who else is around and what dangers lurk.

Next to the farmer is an open trailer with a slaughtered cockroach inside. The bulky man has a tattoo similar to that of the Seductress, a letter *U* behind his ear. He must be another Utopian from this radical cult. And, as he has seen himself, 'hell-bent' on returning Earth to its mid-20th-century self, taking Earth backwards and with it undoing all progress. That noted, VanWest cannot help but think that Paris December 1951 looks a whole lot better than anything he has seen on Earth.

Acknowledging her *U tattoo*, the farmer responds by exchanging a mark of respect before opening a small hatch, which sends a stream of light through the pen. He can't quite hear, but it sounds like she is telling him to 'alert the others'. The Seductress smiles and exits, leaving the farmer to resume his work.

VanWest knows he can't let her escape with the Quantum Accelerator rods, this would risk letting her, or any other Utopian, able to travel through time yet again. Her mission, to 1951 Paris, lucky to have failed. The next might not be so.

With the farmer distracted by his work, VanWest sees his opportunity. Thinking fast, he steers the giant cockroaches towards the farmer, using their fat bodies as cover, allowing him to approach without raising suspicion. As the farmer crouches down to pick up another cockroach leg from the floor, he jumps onto his back and quickly puts him in a chokehold. Even though the farmer is strong, he is no match for an Enforcer. VanWest tightens his hold, rendering him unconscious.

Chapter 9   Leap into the Queen's Nest

VanWest shields his eyes from the sun's glare as he peers outside. Greeting him is a caustic trench of burning rubber, causing his throat to itch and eyes to sting. The smell is unfortunately quite familiar for it is the same as that found on ColaBeers and in all of the Antarctic settlements. Confirming, he is indeed back in the present, back to where the air is barely breathable and quite poisonous without a hazmat mask. Most settlements lack a safety dome to protect the citizens from radioactive radiation and heat. Having been deemed not worth the investment.

Hummm! Whizzing overhead are two Quadrotors, each carrying a large cage on top. They are following, well more stalking and harassing, two sickly-looking elderly citizens dressed in tatty white jumpsuits who trudge slowly along the street, not daring and too exhausted to look up. The Quadrotors are commonly used to oppress the citizens, acting as a constant reminder to behave or else they will be sent to one of the Universal Council's hellish jails. In their system of law, all citizens are treated as if they are criminals, assumed guilty till proven otherwise.

These two bedraggled citizens, a relatively elderly man and woman, are so malnourished that they resemble living skeletons. Their legs bow-shaped and backs bent, they muster all their strength to scavenge for scraps, for something to eat, anything at all. They certainly pose no threat to anyone.

Seeing him staring, they limp over to VanWest, dragging a near-empty food bag, thinly plated with a layer of lead to protect against radiation, along the concrete floor. VanWest notices that the bag displays the label of the Universal Games logo sponsor, *InsectnOut*. The irony doesn't entirely escape him. A brand used to gather scraps by the weakest in society, also used by an Enforcer to win the ultimate prize.

They look bemused at his odd attire, his 1950s Parisian hotel uniform now covered in goo, a mixture of cockroach waste and fodder. With toothless smiles, they stretch out their arms to beg for leftovers, likely assuming him to be a worker from this cockroach farm.

Across the woman's tatty jumpsuit is written: *We Love this City, Queen Elizabeth, Antarctica*. VanWest is relieved, it is indeed the putrid air of Antarctica and it appears he is back in the present, inside Earth's capital city.

VanWest instructs the couple to wait as he goes back into the pen, keen to get them some food. After herding the cockroaches back from the entrance, he pulls a cockroach leg out of the trailer. The couples' wrinkled faces light up as he returns, dropping to their bony knees to thank him. Though its weight is light for VanWest, they struggle to take hold of the leg, which is far too heavy for their malnourished and weakened bodies. Still, they somehow manage, desperate for its sustenance. With grateful smiles, they bid him goodbye and drag their now full bag back down the street.

Flagging the Quadrotors over is not an option for VanWest, for he knows that without his Enforcer uniform he could risk being tasered. Finding himself locked in a holding cell awaiting trial for an unknown number of days, unlikely to be identified immediately. Days he does not have! He needs to get the Quantum Accelerator rods back within 48 hours.

Assumed guilty till proven innocent, Earth's jails are a bleak place. Packed with hundreds of thousands of citizens, many spend upwards of a hundred days awaiting their trial. Eventually, most are convicted of some minor infraction such as being out after curfew or another nonsensical crime of like acting suspiciously, as justification for leaving them in jail so long. For the all-knowing Universal Council is never wrong. Due to the corrupt and inefficient justice system, only those able to bribe jailors or hold any type of influence, such as knowing a Council official or reputed businessman in their district, ever manage to get released early.

Fortunately, the Seductress can't leap straightaway. The Quantum Accelerator rod has a jump-to-jump time of once every 48 hours so he MUST find the useable one. Even though she may technically be able to jump earlier, it's much too unstable to guarantee that she will arrive at the right destination, if at all. Beyond the farm, two-storey warehouses line the road, their lead-plated shutters and walls covered in NEA graffiti. There is no greenery or wildlife, just an eerie silence except for the low hum of the Quadrotors.

He must move fast for other reasons as well, as the sun is soon going to set. From his experiences in ColaBeers, settlements become more dangerous at night. Some places are even abandoned to junkies, rapists, pimps, nightwalkers, and other unsavoury characters. Most of the crime is usually low-level and wouldn't pose a threat to him, a trained Enforcer. However, he doesn't want to draw any unnecessary attention.

Most crimes are committed by those looking for hallucinogenic Papini, called Liquid Blue, some resort to stealing to get their next fix. Other junkies even murder for it. The Universal Council does very little to stop or help them. Instead choosing to lavish their resources on themselves, the Elites, who live far removed from the ordinary citizens and the slums. They simply do not care.

VanWest waits until the Quadrotors are out of sight before hurrying along the street to try and find the Seductress. The wait has been too long and she is nowhere to be seen, likely having disappeared down one of the many side streets or into one of the warehouses. Realising this, and that he still has 48 hours, he decides it best to find an Enforcer station where he can be identified immediately. And, more crucially, do so without risk of being jailed.

A vandalised street sign reads *Mid-City 1 Mile*. Mid-City is the section of each settlement that houses the Enforcer HQ, it's usually in one of the most affluent areas, hence the heavy Enforcer presence. He trusts that Dr King will know what to do. But he also fears being punished for being fooled by the Seductress and, worse still, being robbed of two Quantum Accelerator rods. Hopefully, the news of successfully preventing the Utopians from changing the course of history will appease his liege enough to outweigh his failures. He sticks to the side of the street, moving quickly from shadow to shadow, following the signs towards the twisted skyscrapers in the distance.

As he nears Mid-City, an extremely high-pitched noise - *screech* - comes from all directions. It forces him to his knees in excruciating pain, his hands trying to shield his ears. An intense light follows. Nearly blinded, he is just about able to make out two approaching Enforcers armed with plasma rifles. Alarm sets in as he recognises the weapon's orange line, an indication that 'kill mode' is active. Anticipating the bolt of orange light from the plasma rifle, VanWest instinctively rolls to his right, narrowly dodging the Enforcer's shot as it tears through the pavement.

Spotting a storm drain, he gets up and runs. The patrol androids swarm around the Enforcer, discharging their weapons next. Laser and plasma shots light up the street, which he just about outpaces as he slides inside the drain. He lands in a shallow stream of dirty water filled with a mixture of human faeces and garbage and with it a disgusting stench. *Eeeee!* Shrieks echo along the storm drain, the tunnel-dwellers awoken and sent into a frenzy, tiny bugs scurrying to hide in the small cracks in the wall. Their chirping and hissing sounds quite foreboding.

The siren - *Wah-Wah* - blares as heavy footsteps cause the walls around him to vibrate. VanWest gets back to his feet and scrambles along the narrow sewage tunnel to get away. Wading through the muck, he follows the flow of dirty water. The siren's noise is replaced by even more chirping and hissing. The foul air is more rancid and warmer. He has heard worrying stories of the sewer's dangers, that it is frequently used by the rebels, and knows he must proceed with caution.

After what must be half an hour, he finally reaches the tunnel's end and enters a chamber with a deep pool of incarnadine water in its centre. Suffocating steam evaporates from its surface, drawn up into an air vent above. He can just about make out the writing on a rusty sign, *Aramco Power Station*, next to an equally rusty ladder that leads to the vent's access point. Carefully walking around a narrow ledge that borders the pool, he stretches to grab the bottom rung of the ladder. However, as he grabs hold and pulls himself up, one of the bars snaps, sending his foot into the pool below. *Crunch!* A worrying sound, not a splash as would be expected from water.

He stands in silence, knowing this not to be a good sign. *Chirp-chirp!* An alarming noise fills the chamber, it crescendos as the tiny bugs now flee from the pool. In a panic to escape, they crawl over his body, his ears and mouth. VanWest's hands tremble as he pulls himself up the ladder once again, spitting out the bugs that now clog his throat - *cough*.

Upon reaching the top of the ladder, he notices the chirping noise has changed to a loud humming, which ominously echoes across the chamber, not too dissimilar to that of the farm, but this sound is much more menacing. VanWest slowly turns his head to find a huge cockroach rising up from the water behind him. This one is neither timid nor tame, it's a whole lot meaner looking than its cousins in the farm. It remonstrates angrily, waving its powerful long front legs at him.

By its size, this is one extremely peeved Queen cockroach, likely the mother to all these smaller bugs crawling over him. He has disturbed her nest! She pins him against the wall with her front legs, whilst snapping her pinchers, readying to slice him in half. In a scene strangely reminiscent of the spider in Pytheas's Labyrinth, it looks to be that a giant insect will be his undoing, his end.

Fortune favours him again, there's some unexpected help. Before the Queen snaps at him, a bright bolt of light illuminates the tunnel and strikes her - scattering her black goo across his face and onto the wall behind. Five armed fighters emerge from the adjacent sewer tunnel. To his astonishment one of them is Nurse Rose, from Ward B, recognising her by her frizzy hair and bluish-green emerald ring. She appears to have come out of a nasty firefight. Her right arm is badly burned and face blackened, typical of injuries caused by the blast of an Enforcer's incineration grenade or a patrol android's laser.

'Thank you, you saved me... Nurse Rose is that you'? He calls out to her.

She doesn't seem to recognise him, pointing her rifle confrontationally at his head. Walking closer to get a better look, the air so steamy and his clothing so odd, her face changes, now returning a look of surprise as she lowers her weapon.

'VanWest, is that really you'?

'Yes', he replies.

Slightly taken back by her next question, he doesn't quite know what to answer, 'Are you enemy or friend'?

VanWest hesitates. Taking stock of the situation, he notices that one of the fighters is severely injured and struggles to walk, this woman and these people are rebels, more than that, they are NEA rebels! VanWest finds himself conflicted. The feeling of a warm connection to Nurse Rose, especially after saving him, pitched against his strict Enforcer training. His first thought that of his commandment to destroy all those that defy the Universal. These commandments are his reason to be, to exist, However, he can't destroy them. Unarmed, he reasons that his only option, for now, is to befriend them all.

He replies to Nurse Rose, 'I don't know what to say but let me help your friend up the rusty ladder'!

'Everyone, help LuLu around the pool and to VanWest'! She instructs her fellow rebels as VanWest opens the access point and then helps to lift the injured fighter up.

They enter into another chamber, this one even more full of hot steam, which rises towards a series of turbines, rotating them anti-clockwise. This steam must come from the cooling of the fusion reactors, steam that, in turn, causes the turbines' rotators to spin and charge a number of electric generators. Its power used to keep Queen Elizabeth, its many buildings and installations, running.

'Is this safe'? VanWest asks Nurse Rose.

'Yes, this reactor always runs below capacity', showing him a Geiger counter reading with a low radiation level.

She elaborates, 'Not harmful to humans... We are safe to hide-out here until your pals the Enforcers leave the area'!

'Ok then'! He replies awkwardly. It's for the best, dressed like he is he would risk being shot on the spot.

'Did they not recognise you in your 1950s attire'? Nurse Rose asks sarcastically, with a half-smile, indicating too that she knows of his time-travel mission to the city of light, Paris.

VanWest eyes open wide trying not to act surprised, 'Guess not'!

'I told you, the Universal Council would try to use... ' she stops herself from finishing. She knows that VanWest won't be able to fully understand what she means.

All power stations in the settlements are fusion, creating energy from colliding and fusing together atomic nuclei much in the same way the sun does. It is preferred to other types of power because it produces a large amount of clean energy cheaply. Compared to fission energy in particular, it produces much fewer radioactive particles. However, despite the United Nations Nuclear Deactivation agreement of 2095, that ended their use in powerplants, fission reactors found a new use as nuclear collider propulsion engines, fuelling the rapid growth of long-distance space travel.

The world's then superpowers, intent on winning the space race and gaining more resources, turned a blind eye to its harmful overuse. With money to be made and pride to be won, increasing levels of radiation were ignored. The radiation leakages from spaceships entering and exiting Earth's atmosphere, combined with heavy pollution from mining operations below, soon made all major cities outside of Antarctica uninhabitable. With the Ozone destroyed and the world poisoned, Earth plunged into a medieval-type transitory age for hundreds of years. Humans were forced to migrate and seek refuge in the new Antarctic settlements.

This consolidated power into the hands of the then Grand Council, now Universal Council, who preached a mantra of using advanced technology to improve living conditions and bring about an end to starvation. Saying as they do now, that they work for the progression of man. Well, in truth, for only a few men: 'the Elite'.

Nurse Rose leads the group to the corner of the chamber, coming to a halt before an inactive electric generator and turbine where she opens a panel on her right and pulls down a green lever. *Creak!* It opens a metal hatch, a trapdoor, above their heads.

She instructs everyone, 'Climb inside. They won't be able to detect us in here'.

They crawl through a short tunnel into a den-like, cramped space. A single bulb, the only light, reveals a long, narrow room lined with bloodied and injured people. Surprisingly few are armed, they look like ordinary citizens. VanWest helps the injured fighter through, carefully laying her down. Nurse Rose hands VanWest a flask of purified water, before hurrying over to a makeshift operating table, where a short-haired woman, a surgeon with a bloodstained apron and gloves greets her.

VanWest, wanting a moment to rest, sits down next to the injured fighter. But as he does, a large silver-haired man with dark black eyes charges out. With his fists clenched, he readies to strike, only for Nurse Rose to intercept him, stepping in front.

'Why is he here? You know who he is right'? He scolds Nurse Rose. It's no surprise he knows Captain VanWest. His face continually broadcasted all over the Solar System after his odds-defying triumph at the Universal Red and Blue Games.

'Sparks! Calm down! He helped carry back LuLu. She's badly injured from an incinerator blast... Let's discuss VanWest later', Nurse Rose asks in a soft voice.

This name, hearing it the second time, VanWest realises he has just helped a *Most Wanted,* Lexi LuLu, a Utopian High Priestess. His first thought is what would happen if the Universal Council found out that he aided her? His second what these deviants will do with him, knowing him to be the Universal Council's newest poster boy?

Sparks angrily glares at VanWest and then looks back at Nurse Rose, 'The Enforcer scum came from nowhere, someone must have tipped them off. Dozens of our friends and colleagues have been captured or killed. Was it him'?

'No, it was not. Calm down', Nurse Rose repeats, with a reassuring hand on his shoulder. She adds, 'Sparks, he's under my protection, we must tend to the injured. Let's speak of this later.'

After tending to her own injuries, she grabs a surgical tool and joins the surgeon to help treat LuLu, which VanWest now lifts onto the table. Nurse Rose rolls a primitive cooling device over her arm and shoulder, which soothes her burns, but she has lost a lot of blood, it doesn't look promising.

Inside the den, citizens of all backgrounds and ages hide, having seemingly been attacked without distinction. The youngest victim is barely a few weeks old and the oldest, a grand age for any citizen, over 70. The baby sleeps wrapped in a tiny aluminium foil blanket, held tightly against its distraught mother's bosom. In the corner, he recognises a bag on the floor - it's the one belonging to the old couple who were begging at the cockroach farm, bearing the *InsectnOut* label.

He walks over to have a better look at the old man, who lays stretched out on the floor, semi-conscious. A sad sight indeed. Looking around, he cannot see the old woman he was with, and wonders what has happened to her.

VanWest sits down, watching as the pool of blood grows with each passing hour. The blood drips down the makeshift, and unsanitary, operating table where a tired Nurse Rose and even more exhausted surgeon operate on a seemingly endless stream of victims. The scene reminds him of ColaBeers and, sadly, it does not surprise him that the Enforcers would partake in an attack on citizens so old and young. The wounded old man could barely even walk when he first met him, a threat to no one. VanWest struggles to find any justification for why they are here. Is this for progress?

The smell of antiseptics, cauterisation and blood, combined with this claustrophobic small space, begin to overwhelm VanWest. He wants to leave but dares not ask Nurse Rose. After a few hours, he can't last any longer, his head now pounding and his hands shaking uncontrollably. Only one thought plays in his mind - to get out. Sneaking past Nurse Rose, he crawls through and back into the steamy chamber. It is eerily quiet with the rotators having slowed to an almost dead pace. Sitting on the ground, he takes a few minutes to calm himself and recollect his thoughts.

It's not long before a visibly annoyed Nurse Rose follows behind, her jumpsuit stained brown by the blood and muck of the makeshift operating table.

'Why are you outside? You must come back'! She tells him firmly.

'Why are you allowing me to stay? The NEA does not help their mortal enemy, the Universal Council's Enforcers.'

'You really don't remember, do you'? She answers.

He pauses and stares at her eyes, he thought that she looked familiar. His head begins to swirl as childhood memories start to return. He remembers them together under the stairs, her gentle kiss on his cheek before the matron dragged her away, causing her necklace to snap. The amber stone pendant now tied around his neck. He remembers too that her name means humanity in old Greek.

Looking into her eyes, it's crazy to think how he could have forgotten her, how their destinies have gone in such opposite directions, she an NEA fugitive and he an Enforcer. Only to meet again after so many years, he feels he has reconnected with a long-forgotten, dare he say, friend.

'Iris ... Iris'? He mutters.

'VanWest, yes'! She smiles on hearing him say her name.

He takes off his pendant and presents it to her, 'I believe this is yours'?

Gently wrapping his fingers back over the pendant and pressing it against his chest, she tells him softly, 'Keep it, please. I was already told off for it when I returned home without it. My father was furious, saying it was not of this world and had a unique power. So please, keep it, I do not want any new questions. More so, it IS yours'.

'Thank you', VanWest replies.

'No problem, he only ever gave me one piece of jewellery again after that'! Iris half-jokes, rubbing the bluish-green emerald ring on her finger.

VanWest looks at her electric blue eyes, 'Thank you, you are sweet... It's my only personal possession and means a lot to me, so much more so now'.

'I always hoped it would help you to remember me', she smiles.

They stare at each other for a moment, before VanWest breaks the silence, 'Can I ask, why didn't you tell me who you were in Ward B'?

'Sorry, I could not. It would have put your life at risk. You did not forget me by chance. Your childhood memories were masked for a reason. Telling you... ' she hesitates, she is unsure if or how she can explain.

Taking his hand, 'It would have only overwhelmed. We hadn't seen each other for such a long time, ever since... ', but a blinding orange light lands on them, interrupting her before she can finish.

Chapter 10   A Forgotten Friend

Waaahhhh! A siren blares, reverberating off the pipes and the walls. They are startled to see the inactive turbine connected to the generator beginning to move and speed up. Iris jumps up unsure what is happening, she tries to hit the emergency stop button as screams and shouts of 'help', start to ring out from within. But before she can turn it off, a huge man close to 8-foot tall in blue body armour emerges from the steam and hits Iris in the shoulder with his rifle butt, knocking her down.

Despite VanWest recognising the armour, that of an Enforcer, a red mist transcends over him as he charges, only to find himself also knocked down. Undeterred, he jumps back to his feet. Having fought many bigger Enforcers than himself at the academy, he skilfully kicks the brawny attacker below his right knee, causing him to lose balance and stumble. VanWest does not hesitate, following up he grabs his neck, snapping it effortlessly. The huge Enforcer lies lifeless on the floor.

He can't quite believe what he has done! He has killed a fellow Enforcer! It's about the worst thing he could ever have imagined doing. There is honour among Enforcers and you do not do this.

Waaahhhh! The siren continues to blare as orange light floods the chamber. He helps Iris to her feet, quickly pulling her to another vent a few yards away. She tries to go back, but the screams have already stopped all those inside dead. More Enforcers descend from the metal staircase. Luckily for them, no-one dares to shoot, for any shot could ricochet off the turbine's rotators and hit the pipes, causing a huge explosion that would kill them all. He tears the flimsy iron mesh cover off the vent and they squeeze inside.

A cocky laugh follows them - *ha-ha*, one he has heard many times before. VanWest looks back through the steam to see that it is none other than Alpha. Strangely, he's more interested in posing triumphantly next to the generator than following them, wanting to celebrate his victory. Displaying his dishonourable behaviour yet again.

VanWest helps Iris through the shaft, which leads to the back of the powerplant. They exit onto the street behind an Enforcer patrol vehicle, also known as a police hovercar. The small two-person car is extremely tough, manoeuvrable and fast, reaching speeds over 500mph at sea-level. To achieve this, it uses electromagnetic energy to spin through the air.

A fetid smell greets them, a mixture of burning rubber and something much darker, the stench of roasted flesh. A smell that once experienced never leaves you. He peers over the hovercar to find the harrowing sight of hundreds of dead bodies strewn across the road and pavement, many burnt a charcoal black. The bodies lay in front of a shelter for the aged. These are elderly citizens! They surely posed no threat to anyone!?

A lone Enforcer guards the bodies, waiting for the others to return from the powerplant. VanWest wonders if a massacre similar to that of ColaBeers happened here too, again just collateral damage to the Universal Council, bent on destroying the NEA whatever the human cost may be.

So brutal, it could only have been authorised by the most senior members of the Universal Council. VanWest ponders what the reason could be for the Enforcers swarming the city, turning it upside down to track down every NEA member and accomplice. Could it be that they are aware that the Seductress has returned and has the Quantum Accelerator rod? But who could have informed them and also know of the NEA's hideout?

There must be someone on the inside of the NEA or Utopians, a spy. Either way, it seems they have stepped up efforts to shut down this part of the capital.

VanWest realises that not all the elderly civilians are dead, the lone Enforcer has arrested one who kneels before him with her wrinkled hands above her head. It's the old man's partner, the woman he gave the cockroach leg to. Her tatty grey jumpsuit emblazoned with *We Love this City, Queen Elizabeth, Antarctica*, has been shredded and her face bloodied. Unable to scream, her body is held captive by a restraining forcefield, an Electrolock, which spirals blue around her.

The Electrolock is controlled by the Enforcer's mind, who spins it tighter and tighter, slowly suffocating her. Finally, he relents, dropping her limp body down with her chin smacking against the concrete floor. VanWest knows that he has already broken his commandments by abetting the NEA, but he can't stand idle. Despite risking a charge of treason if caught, he throws himself on top of the Enforcer and immediately puts him in a chokehold until he loses consciousness. This time he is careful not to crush his larynx and kill him like the other in the powerplant. He's already killed one person too many today.

They must flee as quickly as possible. He lifts the Enforcer's head to identify and authorise the use of his hovercar, causing its gullwing doors to swing open. VanWest first helps a clearly concussed, Iris into the passenger seat, the knock by the Enforcer having left a huge bruise on her forehead. He goes to the driver seat and, with him being not the authorised driver, switches to manual controls. A joystick juts out from the dashboard into his hands.

VanWest thrusts it forward to speed away from the scene as fast as possible. He looks over at Iris who sits in deep silence beside him, her eyes filled with despair and sorrow, so many of her friends have been killed today. Taking the highway above the main road, he does well to navigate through the black smoke billowing from burning buildings. Following the route towards Mid-City, he switches to incognito mode to avoid any radar, the vehicle now appearing as any other flying car.

It won't be long before the knocked-out Enforcer wakes up or is found, so he keeps at the maximum speed of 500mph. He figures that the best place to hide is right under the nose of the Enforcer HQ in Mid-City, and despite helping Iris, he is still undecided on what to do next. Wondering if he should bring himself in, if not her as well. Now both '*a traitor and a hero*', he must decide, which side he is on.

The internal conflict great. Whilst friend is not a concept he understands too well, he knows he is fond of her. Now far from the powerplant, his adrenaline level begins to return to normal. He knows too he must stay alert. If caught, his notoriety and heroics in winning the Games will do little to protect him. In fact, being this year's poster boy could even make his situation a whole lot worse!

Ahead, a large holosign, *Demron*, illuminates the grey skyline, pointing VanWest towards a possible place to stay undetected; a small diamond-shaped motel with a silver roof and a honeycomb of black pods, small living quarters. Demron doesn't just do motels, it covers an array of products and services, from clothing to leisure facilities, and can be found in all human settlements. They are best known for their innovative and easy fitting jumpsuit, which comfortably protects against harmful radiation.

Demron's owners are the infamous Elites called the Huberts. Owners of the food chain *InsectnOut*, VanWest's helmet sponsors in the Universal Games, given to him in thanks for saving the head of the family during his first tour as a newly graduated Enforcer. Their involvement with the Universal Council nowadays is said to be minimal. Their vast riches and influence allowing their companies to operate with relative anonymity, free of restraint as well as competition. For this reason, its motels remain one of the only places not requiring stringent registration and vetting procedures for guests. Less red tape is good for business as they say. And therefore, a place VanWest can use as a safe house.

With Iris now asleep, he quietly parks the hovercar inside a metal container, trusting that its thick metal walls will keep the vehicle from being detected. Lifting Iris out, he carries her two floors up to the closest available black pod, careful to conceal his face in case a Quadrotor passes by.

Although he doesn't have any currency on him, Demron luckily takes pints of healthy blood as payment. But he must hope that his exposure to the powerplant's radiation hasn't reduced its worth. He places his forearm into the blood payment device, returning with the cost of a night's stay at a hefty pint. The human body only has 10 and there's no late checkout included. His blood scores *Radiation Free, Accepted.*

With so many suffering from radiation poisoning, there is great demand for healthy blood to detoxify. Demand is driven even higher by the Elites, who consume it in huge quantities for aesthetic purposes, - healthier hair and fingernails - depleting the supply and driving up its price. Blood can be made in labs but organic, antibody-rich blood, is preferred. The synthetic blood, whilst cheaper, is still unaffordable for most and in short supply.

The inside of the pod is basic. Furnished with an aluminium foil blanket and a hole for a toilet, a far cry from the luxury of a SCC Hypersphere pod. Its shape hexagonal and cramped, about three metres long and two metres wide and tall. This Mid-City low-cost accommodation designed for traders that seek shelter and respite; not only from the radiation and heat but the thieving junkies and treacherous night, Quadrotors, and the frequent dust storms.

VanWest lays next to Iris, lifting her head gently upon the thin pillow and removing her worn-out boots. Seeing that she is shivering from shock, VanWest holds her in his arms to warm her up. Exhausted, having ventured from one high octane drama to the next, he drifts to sleep.

An earlier vision returns. Back on the sand, he stands in an arena surrounded by spectators. A few meters away is Alpha holding his laser dagger against the slender neck of the frizzy-haired woman he now knows to be his childhood friend Iris. Alpha looks up, waiting for a decision from a bald-headed man with a white goatee in a gilded stand - the Universal Council's leader Dr King. Wearing a ceremonial toga and gold-leafed corona just like in the Universal Games, he stretches out his right arm with his fist clenched. Dr King's aura that of a Roman Emperor in a Gladiator's tournament.

VanWest finds himself frozen and unable to move, watching as Dr King finally signals back to Alpha, his thumb pointing down. *Da-da-dum!* Drums pound in unison as Alpha pulls Iris's head back and cuts her throat.

Gasp! VanWest awakens back in the pod. Iris, thankfully, is still in his arms, her neck as perfect and slender as before. Outside the pod, he notices footsteps and a short bald man in a tatty jumpsuit hovering around. His big green eyes stare at the pod's door. At first, VanWest thinks it to be a homeless man coming to beg but the man knocks on the door in a curious manner, in bursts of three - *tap-tap-tap* - as if relaying a secret code. Something tells him that this man is not a threat, and turns the glass transparent.

The man smiles broadly, 'Hello! VanWest, is that you? My, my, have you grown'!

'Sorry do I know you'? A puzzled VanWest replies.

The knocks have awoken Iris, who comes to the door. Giving VanWest a reassuring stroke on his back, she opens the door and with a big smile covering her face hugs the man, 'Hello Papa'!

Chapter 11 A Traitor and a Hero

Papa!? VanWest wonders if this short bald man could be Mad Newton. Remembering Dr King's description and interface, and remembering who Iris is, it most likely is so! The man exchanges a warm embrace with his daughter. She must have sent a communication during the night with their location, that or her father was able to track them down.

'My love, I'm glad I found you! Enforcer activity has increased threefold since last night. Many lives lost', Mad Newton informs, his expression turning more sombre. Both Iris and VanWest are not surprised to hear this, having witnessed it themselves.

He continues, taking hold of his arm, 'VanWest! Dear VanWest! Thank you so very much for saving my beloved daughter. I'm Doctor VonHelmann'. He adds with a hint of amusement, 'Yes, that same man their propaganda machine ignominiously dubs Mad Newton'.

VanWest momentarily silent, replies, 'I thought so'.

'Do you not remember me'? Mad Newton asks.

He does seem familiar, and not just because he is featured weekly in the *Most Wanted*. VanWest has seen him before in his dreams, his visions although less haggard looking.

'Don't worry if you can't... Thy childhood memories have been meddled with. It hides thy truth, thy purpose and existence, the secrets of thy origins', Mad Newton's expression changing to that of pity.

'I don't understand', a surprised VanWest replies. 'VanWest... You should not have meddled in Paris'.

'I was sent to stop you, your evil mission to distort the time continuum. Are you not trying to change our present? Take us backwards and lose all progress'? VanWest asks in a firm tone.

'Do not be so easily used', Mad Newton replies, his tone still that of pity.

'Can you not fix this world without changing the past'? VanWest rebuts, defensively.

'No! The Universal Council has become too powerful and corrupt. The creation of CERN is one of a few seismic events that ended the dream of Utopia by the 21st-century Philosopher Hans Ashtar forewarned those in the late 20th century not to let machines guide our behaviour, our moral decisions. But alas they took no notice'.

Mad Newton pauses, his tone now more that of annoyance, 'VanWest, do you not observe all around you? Does it not feel odd? Unnatural'?

Iris adds, 'The citizens are controlled by machines, do you not notice the cyborgs, Quadrotors, patrol androids, spaceships and holoscreens. Only by going back to our past can we save the present'.

VanWest, finding it hard to wrap his head around the logic, remains unconvinced, 'There must be an alternative'?

As a well-trained Enforcer, he can detect when someone is concealing information. He feels Mad Newton is hiding something, his tone changing back to one of pity again as his hand moves away, 'Dear VanWest, well... maybe once there was a green technology, a box, but thy Council destroyed that too'.

VanWest wants to press further but before he can do so, Mad Newton removes a green hexagon-shaped chip from his pocket and hands it to him, 'This will unmask thy lost memories, thy world, thy existence. Insert this into thy ear node after we leave. Fear not it to be found, our top hacker has masked thee from the Universal's machines'.

VanWest accepts. He feels though a sense of loathing, fearful of what else he has forgotten and what it may do to him. Inserting it, he does not yet start the interface. Mad Newton pats him reassuringly on his shoulder, 'In less than 34 hours a NEW Beginning will start for us all. I want you to join us'!

'What is this New Beginning'? An already bewildered VanWest asks.

Mad Newton opens his hand, he has the silver Quantum Accelerator rod!

'To return with me to the time before Utopia was lost. I urge you to take thy opportunity to join and help us. To trust in Utopia... Thy gifted mind sees our future. One that you can help us to shape. Ling Ling has returned us the rod'.

A concerned VanWest is not happy to hear this, neither is he glad to hear his mind being called 'gifted' by now two doctors. He struggles to differentiate one from the other, so similar they are in manner, speech, stature and background. Each espouses their own point of view as the correct one.

Iris adds, 'We took great risk to meet you in Ward B. This chip gives you back your memories, who you are, the truth. You can now make an informed decision... I hope one to help us'.

Mad Newton explains further, 'Thy ability... I masked from the Universal as long as I could. Play the chip and decide'!

Mad Newton expression changes as he looks back at the grey sky, turning to that of concern. Now handing VanWest a low-tech square communicator, 'The Universal are searching everywhere. Stay low in Mid-City for the next 33 hours, closer to the time we will send you the coordinates via this communicator to our underground base. A final leap and New Beginning starts'.

'Affirmative... ok', VanWest forgetting himself and answering as an Enforcer.

'Trust in Utopia'!

Iris looks sad to leave VanWest, kissing him warmly on the cheek just like when they were children before following her father into the street where they crawl inside a storm drain. As if Mad Newton had sensed it, Quadrotors appearing in the skies as they disappear.

VanWest notices that his hands are trembling again, a sign that he has come to understand that something is about to happen.

Before he can step back into the pod, a sharp noise - *screech* - forces him to his knees and his square communicator from his hands, falling from the deck and smashing on the ground below. An intense and blinding orange light follows.

The Enforcers are here! Their heavy footsteps cause the deck to shake violently as the siren's dissonant noise increases even further - *screech*. VanWest covers his ears in anguish, wishing it to stop.

'Hands up, roachtard'!

The blinding light dims to reveal the gleeful killer Captain Alpha alongside numerous Enforcer patrol androids. Dust swirls up around them as a large ship decloaks, it's the SCC-400. A greenish-blue bolt of light follows, hitting the tarmac and transporting down Colonel Cornelius in full body armour. VanWest tries to call out but one of the patrol androids hits him with a Taser amplifier as a stinging jolt of electricity forces him down on his knees. Smashing his head against the railing of the deck, causing his body to spasm, and eyes to close.

He finds himself naked on a cold floor where a yellow-eyed and reptile-like man stares at him with interest. It is an Inspector he knows well, the Interrogator from ColaBeers. His white lab coat is stained with blood and sleeves singed black. VanWest tries to lift his badly burned and reddened hands up but cannot. Trapped in a container of sorts, he is stuck. A man is watching him, bald-headed with a long white goatee - it is Dr King. He tries to call out, only for light to fill his container. Flames cover and melt VanWest's skin. *Agh!* The pain worse than any he has ever experienced before.

He awakens on a cold floor, now surrounded by electric bars that pulsate systematically, fading briefly before shining brightly again. His body no longer singed or his skin melted; he is dressed in black prison garb. It all feels like a dream. Through the bars, someone is watching and moving closer, he can make out two menacing and small yellow eyes staring at him. A déjà vu as the pulsating bars fade, he sees the small beady eyes belong to the Interrogator. This is not good! His white lab coat is stained with blood and sleeves singed black just like he saw before. Was it a dream? VanWest tries to speak but cannot. The Interrogator steps inside, carrying with him a silver chrome box.

Two Elite patrol androids follow next, their limbs elongating towards him. VanWest doesn't know where he is or what is happening, he tries to shuffle back, but there is nowhere to escape to. They aggressively pin him against the floor and strip his clothes off, VanWest too shocked to scream or resist.

The Interrogator wears his amber stone pendant, goading him with it, 'Ss-so pretty, pretty'!

The androids force his mouth open, inserting a small silver object inside. VanWest feels a weird sensation, something spiderlike is slowly crawling across his tongue and then scurries down his throat. VanWest can feel its razor-sharp legs twisting and turning as it passes through his oesophagus. The pain is unbearable as it extends and wraps its long legs around his spine.

Agh! The Interrogator smiles, he's enjoying VanWest's pain like a weird fetish and sticks his tongue out to lick his lips. His whole demeanour and posture that of a snake.

He goads him, his voice hissing, 'Weak, weak. It hurts, hurts you so bad, bad... Tell me plan. So pain stop, ss-stop'!

VanWest knows by now this is all very real, he is being punished. 'This plan', the Universal Council must know of his meeting with Iris and Mad Newton. *Agh!* The pain makes him squirm, his body contorting, it feels like every part of his body is being stabbed again and again. He knows the Interrogator's methods all too well. The worst thing he could do is admit any wrongdoing or admit that he helped these high-profile Utopians - this would bring not only certain death but also more torture.

He channels his Enforcer mindfulness training as taught by Master Jiang at the academy - a professor in philosophy, self-defence, mind conditioning and strengthening. Physical pain is but an illusion, existing only if one chooses for it to exist. Appointed by Dr King, after spending centuries as an Elite guard, Master Jiang educates the Enforcers on mindfulness. How to separate their mind from their bodies, alongside other lessons such as endlessly reciting and writing out the Universal commandments.

The mind strengthening classes were tough but also very effective. VanWest remembers one such lesson where Master Jiang used an ancient method, originating from the ancient art of Kung-Fu, to teach discipline. Forcing the class to squat down and balance a boiling hot cup of tea on each knee. One had to remain still for half an hour, if one cup were to spill and drop, usually scolding one's leg and feet, one would have to restart. Soon the physical pain of the hot tea scolding one's knee and foot became irrelevant against the psychological pain of stopping and starting. Hence, disciplining one's physical self, in turn, helped one's mental self. For VanWest, the trick was to remain in a trance and to forget the cups were even there.

VanWest's resistance doesn't surprise the Interrogator for he knows of the Enforcer's training and exceptional resistance to torture and pain. Rather it piques his interest; he enjoys the challenge of coming up with what to try next. Thus, he decides on something even more brutal.

Recalling the spider, the Interrogator instructs his androids to take an exhausted VanWest out of the cell. Dragged along the floor, he can see the other cells, through the red pulsating bars are many badly bruised and reddened bodies. The Interrogator can't resist stopping to look at one. Licking his lips, he gleefully watches as a woman is struck by an electric bolt.

He-he! Sniggering as her body is sent into a spasm, rolling and twisting across the floor. VanWest can see her eyes fade as her twitching slows, he watches the life draining from her body. He fears that the Interrogator has stopped here for a reason, that a similar fate awaits him. Will he die this way too?

The Androids drag him further down the corridor and through a door into the centre of a chamber surrounded by panes of frosted glass. As they leave, the panes become transparent. It is a container he has seen before, maybe it was a dream, another vision, where he was set on fire. VanWest looks across to find Colonel Cornelius watching, seeing a strong hint of concern etched across his face, his forehead wrinkled and eyes sullen. Dr King is there too.

'Boy! Make this easier on yourself. Lest you did not know, we have proof you aided and abetted a MOST Wanted and his daughter. I warned you, did I not say this woman was evil'? Dr King scolds.

He continues, his eyes scowling, 'Sofia Iris VonHelmann. Not only this, YOU let her father, lest I need to say the MOST wanted criminal, Mad Newton, escape! You know the Universal is all-knowing. What were you thinking? Dumb boy! Easily fooled and gullible, I shouldn't be surprised. Your kind'!

VanWest too weakened and tired to respond, wonders what he means by 'your kind'.

The Colonel looks at VanWest willing him on to respond with some sort of explanation, anything, even taking the brave decision to come to his aid. He interjects, 'If I may my liege... Captain VanWest has been a top Enforcer. He may have an explanation for all this'.

There is much honour among the Enforcers, VanWest feels guilty and ashamed for letting his Colonel down. He is lost for words, unable to explain himself. The momentary silence is interrupted by the Interrogator's giggles as he goads VanWest again by licking his amber stone pendant, very much enjoying the sight of his anguish.

The Colonel looks down and away, allowing the Interrogator to introduce his next painful torture. 'Welcome! Welcome to sun sssun tanning salon. It open, open. *He-he*! Please, please forgive me, me so clumsssy, ever so so clumsssy, clumsssy. Turn up high, high. *He-he*'!

The glass panels of the container transform once again, lighting up, its heat unbearable. VanWest screams in agony; he can feel himself being set alight as his skin turns bright red and blisters. Master Jiang's training is not enough to repress the excruciating pain.

'Bravo! Bravo! Tan-tan'! The Interrogator taunts and sings.

Dr King, no longer scowling, gestures to the Interrogator to pause the torture. Impressed by his resistance, he says 'Boy! The Universal has engineered and trained you well, lest it must be said, your gullibility lets you down. A mere human would have begged for mercy and a quick death long ago. But then again, you are not quite that'.

His tone a little more forgiving, 'Boy, are you so gullible? So easy to fool... Explain yourself'?

VanWest musters all his strength to finally give an answer. His throat dry and his voice hoarse, he comes up with a plausible excuse, partly a lie, 'My liege, it was part of my mission. I needed to gain their trust to gather intel. This after I stopped Jaaro and saved our present. The Seductress though was too cunning'.

Dr King gives a half-smile, 'Yes, the Seductress is quite so. Explain further, to gain their trust? Intel'?

'Yes, my liege... It led... me to Mad Newton', VanWest explains, his voice croaking.

'Go on'! Dr King encourages. The Colonel discreetly nodding too.

'My liege, it worked... But the Quadrotors outside of the motel came too late. Not all is lost, I have intel on Mad Newton's plan', VanWest offers, hoping to barter it in exchange for his life.

Dr King is intrigued, staying silent to hear more. In contrast, the glee and excitement of the Interrogator evaporates, who stops licking his lips and sits down.

'The leap is happening in a subterranean base... A final leap, a New Beginning'.

Dr King stares at him before replying, 'VanWest, my boy... I'm going to give you the benefit of the doubt! This is most useful! You have always proven to be a loyal and skilled Enforcer. Lest I did not acknowledge... I give credit where credit is due... stopping that deviant Jaaro from changing time and chasing the Seductress out of 1951'.

VanWest replies obsequiously, but he is surprised, those are details he didn't share. 'Thank you, thank you, my liege. I am but your humble servant'. He continues, perhaps oversharing, 'The Seductress got away with the... with the rod'.

'Ah my boy, fear not. The Universal is all-knowing. Lest you did not know, the Seductress, yes, she has risen to Mad Newton's inner circle'!

VanWest looks up, shocked and surprised, by his response. Is she a spy?

Dr King smiles, 'By killing this higher-ranked deviant Jaaro and returning him the rod, she has taken his place. Our plan coming together perfectly'.

An alarmed VanWest cannot help but ask, 'My liege, I do not understand. She gave Mad Newton the rod'!?

'Fear not, we have his dented prototype. Our Head of Science, Dr Schuurman, fixes it. Lest you had not known, Ling Ling 'The Seductress' we control, our inside agent. By giving Mad Newton this working rod, she has won his trust. This so-called new beginning now a trap, to lure the Utopians, deviants, into his bunker. There we, well I mean you, will strike'! Dr King explains his cunning plan, looking very proud of himself.

'My liege, I'm very glad to hear this. Please know this, I am the most loyal and most devoted of Enforcers, always adhering to the Universal commandments. I thank you and continue to serve and work for the progression of man and the Universal; to serve without question and with utter devotion'.

VanWest, being as obsequious as he can possibly be, does his best to act pleased and to hide his concern for Iris. Mentally and physically drained, he winces in pain with every word he speaks.

'Tell me, your visions, what do they show now? Is there still a wreck'? Dr King asks with a slight hint of anxiety.

VanWest ponders what to say. It seems this 'hacker' that Mad Newton mentioned has indeed managed to stop the Universal Council from reading his mind. Finding it hard to continue speaking, he forces himself, 'Only but one, the executions of those deviants by the Universal Council. This evil woman will be executed at the hands of Captain Alpha'.

'Excellent! Be it better you to kill this evil woman. But Captain Alpha makes sense', Dr King smiles, indicating he wants more from VanWest.

'Of course, my liege', VanWest replies.

Dr King's eyes narrow, his forehead frowning, 'My boy, lest you forget, this evil woman, do not let her make your mind weak. She is bent, unbalanced by the ideologies of her father. This gullibility you are susceptible to... you must understand she cannot be saved. We will strengthen your mind. We will help you to kill her'.

Taking cue, the Colonel interjects, 'My liege, the program is ready'.

'Yes, thank you, my liege', VanWest replies, relieved to have survived this and that the torture has finally ended.

The tanning salon glass panes change once again, this time spraying his body with foam, reversing the damage from the burns and removing most of the pain. VanWest, now able to move, bows low to Dr King to give his thanks and respect.

'Mad Newton's bunker, his hiding place, is part of your mission tomorrow. Use it to rebuild your reputation. Prove once and for all your allegiance to the Universal Council by killing Mad Newton's daughter! Bring me Mad Newton ALIVE in time for Judgment Day. Do not fail me'! Dr King warns him in a firm tone.

'My liege, I relish this opportunity. I will not fail you', VanWest doing his best to not show any empathy and worry for Iris.

The Colonel asks, 'My liege, if I may'?

After a nod from Dr King, he turns to VanWest, 'Captain, the briefing commences at ten hundred hours. You will join Captain Alpha's squad at the command centre. Joining you will be two bunker specialists to devise a plan to enter their well-guarded base. Now heal and begin Master Jiang's convalescing and mind strengthening program. You will have a few hours to revise the commandments as your wounds heal'.

VanWest replies obediently, 'Yes, Colonel. Affirmative'.

Dr King ends the conversation, 'Time is of the essence, their New Beginning draws closer. You will strike before their scheduled leap between seventeen and eighteen hundred hours. Be ready'!

The Interrogator's Elite patrol androids grab hold of him, steering him out of the torture chamber and away. The Interrogator still holds his amber stone pendant, licking it as he leaves.

VanWest shrewd excuse and explanation has saved his life! He exits mostly in one piece to a pod on *C deck* to undergo Master Jiang's Hypersphere program. He exhales deeply. It doesn't feel like a victory as he tries to suppress thoughts of Iris and her safety. Inside the pod, his body shudders as the convalescing commences, quickly entering him into a dream state.

The sequence takes him back to the Enforcer academy, back to his first philosophy class. A class taught by his professor Master Jiang. The professor forces them to repeat the Universal's three commandments, which he writes with chalk on a blackboard.

Commandment 1. To serve without question the Universal Council
Commandment 2. To work for the progression of man and the Universal
Commandment 3. To destroy all those who defy the Universal Council

Master Jiang hands VanWest the white chalk crayon and instructs him to continue writing the commandments out. VanWest does as he is instructed, writing them until he cannot remember anything else.

Several hundred lines later, VanWest awakens back in the elevator looking at his reflection. He's now dressed in a standard-class Enforcer uniform, his Moggle X lenses and hazmat mode activated. His body, apart from his bloodshot eyes, shows no visible signs of his torture. As if it was just one long, terrible nightmare.

VanWest's mind has been refocused, his conflicting thoughts gone. His only thought, how best he can serve his Masters, fulfil his commandments, including to destroy all those who defy the Universal Council. It's 10 in the morning, ten hundred hours, and it is time for the mission briefing with Captain Alpha and Colonel Cornelius.

The elevator travels sideways to collect the Colonel who looks happy to see him, 'Captain VanWest, good morning'!

'Good morning, Colonel Cornelius', VanWest replies mechanically and bows slightly.

'Are you ready for today'? The Colonel asks.

Staring blankly at the Colonel, he answers, 'Yes, Colonel Cornelius'. Reciting the commandments, 'I serve without question the Universal Council. I work for the progression of man and the Universal. I will destroy all those who defy the Universal Council'.

The Colonel looks at him with concern, 'I'm sorry for what happened... VanWest, I never was able to thank you for winning the Games'. Revealing a worrying detail, he adds in a low voice, 'I owe you honour on behalf of all the Enforcers, if it weren't for your gift and victory, we would have all been replaced by Space Soldiers by now'.

Chapter 12   To Serve the Universal

The elevator transports them to the top of the SCC-400, into a dome-shaped room on the command deck. The ship sits hidden from view on top of the Enforcer HQ in Mid-City, cloaked to remain discreet. Its panoramic views are truly breathtaking, giving an uninterrupted 360-degree view of the capital Queen Elizabeth. The deck perfect for surveillance and to strategise.

On the Westside is the district of the Elites. Large buildings line the streets, many surrounded with their own magnetic dome, opaque and tinted to hide and protect those inside from the outside world and elements. There are several skyscrapers, the most impressive of, which is the Vitali Sun Terra: a humongous twisted green tower whose design represents a rarity amongst the plethora of grey, anti-radiative painted, concrete buildings that make up the majority of the capital. Built after receiving special approval from the Universal Council a couple of centuries ago. It belongs to a reclusive Oligarch Marcus Vitali who constructed the tower in memory of a child he lost. He wanted to create a community for the descendants of Elites, to protect them against the dangers of the outside world, fully self-sufficient, so its residents never need to leave.

The structure is a mini-city, built up of a neuron-like collection of towers that interconnect and reach up over 700 meters high. Each neuron is co-dependent on the other. Everything can be found inside; residents live and work there, sharing amenities and facilities such as pools, theatres, healthcare and parks, as well as workspaces. It even has its own renewable energy; including solar panels and wind turbines and collects methane from human excrement and food waste.

Citizens of Queen Elizabeth refer to these people as 'the descendants of Vitali'. Few have ever seen these residents, leading to many tales being told. That the people are severely obese and pasty-skinned hobbit-like hermits or that these people cannot even walk, requiring wheelchairs and transport tubes to get around the massive building.

On the Eastside the views are, one might say, not so aesthetically pleasing, more plainly put, very grim. The Universal Council raids have not helped, leaving the landscape and many of its buildings a charred and twisted mess. The Universal's most recent incursion, the gruesome massacre in and around the nuclear fission powerplant, has left a large section smouldering and covered in a thick blanket of black smoke.

Some of the smoke has drifted to the capital's edge, shrouding the relatively low-tech glasshouse plantations of the green and radioactive resistant soya beans. The citizens will be hoping it clears soon, relying on the soya beans for protein, especially for those that cannot afford or find cockroach meat scraps. Without sunlight, there will be no photosynthesis, and some may even starve. Soya beans, fed by a network of canals, are one of only a few crops able to grow and make use of the capital's heavily toxic water supply. The water passes through the plantations before emptying out into the ocean, the Weddell Sea.

In the middle of the command centre are several circular green sonic chairs facing towards a large spherical 4D holomap. Seated, and interfaced with it, are figures that VanWest has come to know a little too well of late: Dr King, Commissioner Ming, and, as he was told, Captain Alpha. There are also two well-known experts in bunker infiltration, Captain Dell and Captain Zheng. Their missions have become a thing of legend in the Enforcer academy amongst the students and professors alike. Indeed, VanWest had to master their technique of breaking into locked and blockaded rooms, known as the ZhengDell, before he could graduate. This involved sending a series of shots in opposite directions and then forward to protect from a side assault.

The Colonel and VanWest take their seats and join the interface, instantly taking them inside the map, a 4D blueprint of the Utopian's base, which extends several floors below the surface. Rotating clockwise, it reveals more detail, highlighting a path through each level. VanWest notices the surface level looks very familiar, it is the cockroach farm he leapt into! It makes sense, the Seductress returning here from 1951 Paris and unwittingly taking him to the NEA's secret bunker base.

As an agent and spy for the Universal Council, it isn't surprising she shared this location with them, having likely been picked up soon after leaving the farm. Thinking back, VanWest wonders if he missed the Seductress giving the farmer the working Quantum Accelerator rod. Or maybe she left it to be collected later in one of the cockroach pens.

With the return of the Quantum Accelerator rod, the Seductress must have earned Mad Newton's full trust just as Dr King had hoped. The cockroach farm is a perfect hiding place for a Utopian HQ, their comings and goings disguised as farm work, the selling of meat products an excellent cover. The map augments the surface area of the bunker base, focusing in on a black, high capacity industrial furnace located near the cockroach pens. The furnace incinerates and converts-agricultural waste into electricity.

Commissioner Ming leads the briefing, 'Armed with the information from our agent, be sure we have surveyed their base in great detail'.

The interface zooms inside the black furnace as the Colonel takes over, 'Captain Alpha, your squadron must infiltrate with lightning-fast speed through this furnace and enter into the bunker below. See the trap doors? Make sure you time it RIGHT, every 20 seconds flames shoot from within'.

Captain Alpha responds enthusiastically, pleased to have been appointed squadron leader, 'Affirmative, Colonel'!

The Colonel continues, 'Pay close attention, everyone... The agent will load a Trojan virus to corrupt their security systems, allowing you time to infiltrate, pass through. You MUST be fast, speed is of the essence, if not Mad Newton will leap into the past and alter our present'!

Dr King interjects, warning, 'Lest I must say again, time is running out. We expect there to be many Utopians readying'.

The hologram changes from the bunker layout to that of a series of faces - VanWest recognises some of them from his earlier mission to 1951 Paris and the *Most Wanted* list. More than anyone else, he recognises the frizzy-haired Iris. An internal conflict plays on his mind. His mind is telling him to kill her his heart telling him to protect her. This 'New Beginning' has indeed brought together many high-ranking Utopians. Mad Newton's entire inner circle must be there.

After Master Jiang's HyperSphere sequence, his mind focuses on one thought: the commandment to destroy all those who defy the Universal Council. Even if this includes Iris. He MUST kill them all.

The Colonel activates the node behind his ear, inserting a red diamond chip with the secret base's coordinates. Returning with the layout of the third-level basement floor. 'Squad! Our inside agent will rendezvous with you at this level, follow this path from the furnace. If all goes to plan, the agent should be waiting. Identifying herself by the letters T-I-T-O. I repeat T-I-T-O... Affirmative'?

'Yes, Colonel. Affirmative'! The squad replies.

He continues, 'In the unlikely scenario that she doesn't appear, assume the worst. That a portal is already open. Charge straight in! Affirmative'?

'Yes, Colonel. Affirmative'! The squad repeats.

The 4D hologram map shifts to the outside of the farm as Captain Zheng takes over. In succession, the map highlights several possible entrances into the building. Captain Zheng systematically crossing out each:

- *the access point on the rooftop* - impeded by a razor-sharp electric wire
- *the large sliding hangar door at the back* - several hidden sensory turrets
- *the front entrance blocked by giant farm cockroaches and goo* - too slow

With all entrances crossed out in red, *High Risk Of Delay*, Mad Newton would likely get a heads up if they were to approach, able to leap before they arrive. This 48-hours delay is for a stable leap - a random, erratic one can happen at any time.

Dr King interrupts, 'Lest we forget, time is of the essence. Zero hour is fast approaching until the time the Quantum Accelerator becomes sufficiently stable for a targeted location and date. Once so, the Utopians' New Beginning commences'.

Captain Zheng nods and shifts to the east side of the farm where another entrance is highlighted green. Zooming in on an access point that empties wastewater into the water system, a green line showing how it is collected at the waterworks facility nearby. Behind this access point is a water tank, filled with hundreds of creatures, their bodies elongated and cylindrical, which twist and swim up and down. VanWest activates his Moggle X and Wiki to get more detail on the creatures, downloading the file, *Electric Eels*.

It details how the hardy species is capable of delivering large electric shocks, swimming up to the surface every 10 minutes to breathe in oxygen from the air. Unlike the cockroaches, the eels are far too valuable for consumption. By harnessing their electric shocks, they provide an additional source of power, further helping the Utopians to stay off the capital's energy grid, avoiding suspicion and probing by the Enforcers that regularly investigate anomalies.

The hologram map zooms in on the eels, showing how the energy is harnessed. Every twenty minutes, a giant claw incites them to act defensively, generating an electric shock in unison. This electricity is then collected via thousands of small conductors connected to the tank and stored in a battery. More importantly, the tank is a way for the squad to enter into the farm.

The 4D hologram changes and shifts to this waterworks' facility, approximately 100 meters away, where Captain Zheng points at the green line, naming it *Phase 1*, showing a path along the pipes to the farm's access point. The waterworks houses several large storage tanks, shaped like inverted cones.

Captain Zheng explains, 'Squad. Every few hours the eels rest, the next rest period starts at sixteen hundred and finishes at eighteen hundred. This leaves an unguarded entrance into the base through the tank. Once we reach the tank, phase 2 commences! Copy that'?

Captain VanWest and Dell reply, 'Affirmative'.

'In phase 2, we must swim through the eel tank to the exit here. Close to the black furnace. When we reach it, phase 3 commences. Copy that'?

'Affirmative, Captain', Captain VanWest and Dell reply again.

'I'm not a roachtard, got it... Captain', Alpha confirms too, acting slightly offhand, displeased that he is not leading this part of the briefing.

'Captain, you will be a roachtard if you rattle those eels, swim slowly'! Zheng stresses, sensing Alpha's impulsive nature.

Captain Dell takes over the next part of the infiltration into the bunker. 'Ok squad, during phase 2 and 3 a Trojan virus will bring down the camera system and allow us to reach the black furnace undetected. Listen up, in phase 2 the danger is electric shock, 3 being incinerated like the cockroach fodder'!

The holomap zooms back to the black furnace in order to show its entrance levers, as Captain Dell continues, 'See this first lever to open the shutter, this only gives access to the furnace'.

He pauses, 'Once through, watch closely here, there is another lever by this red panel but it's not easy to get to. Flames shoot through the furnace every 20 seconds. Captain Zheng and I will hurry to pull down this second lever. Enter the bunker complex fast to commence phase 4. You MUST follow in the next window. Move as quickly as possible to not get fried. Copy that'?

VanWest acknowledges once more, 'Yes, Captain'.

Alpha replies with an arrogant smile, 'As clear as night and day'!

Zheng responds sarcastically, 'Thank you for your patience Captain Alpha'!

Dell continues, working in sync with Zheng, the interface moving to the third level down. 'Perfect planning is key... Once regrouped, phase 4, we proceed from this level to basement level three. We then wait for phase 5, for our inside agent to open this locked door here. T-I-T-O, we storm in'!

'Blast them to cockroach goo', Alpha adds enthusiastically.

'Note, hostile count estimated at between twenty and twenty-five'.

Dr King, watching intently, interjects in a firm voice, 'Lest I must say again, kill all but Mad Newton. The Universal Council will make an example of him'.

'Yes, my liege'! The squad answers.

Captain Dell finishes, 'The estimated time of their leap is between seventeen and eighteen hundred'. That's 5 in the afternoon, not too far away from now.

The Colonel summarises, 'The Trojan virus' loop is only temporary. That's 5 minutes to complete phase 2 and 3. Phase 4 we wait for the agent. Phase 5 code word T-I-T-O we storm. Affirmative'?

'Yes, Colonel. Affirmative'! All reply.

Dr King ends the interface on a sobering note, 'Lest you do not know, this operation must be a success. Failure is not an option. Serve the Universal Council well, do not let thee down. You represent the Enforcers; you are their very best. Succeed and you will be rewarded'.

The briefing ends and the squad, along with the Colonel, reply together, 'Yes, my liege'.

It's now 2 noon, fourteen hundred hours. Pointing at the elevator, the Colonel barks, 'ATTENTION! LET'S GO! DECK A, ARMOURY!

As they hurry to the elevator, Dr King pulls VanWest aside, handing him a new Quantum Communicator, 'My boy, once you capture Mad Newton and kill his evil daughter, you will finally become an Elite. If anyone should leap, remember to follow'!

VanWest bows to Dr King, mechanically replying, 'My liege. I am your servant, I work for the progression of man and the Universal Council, be assured that I will serve you well'.

VanWest, Dr King giving him permission to proceed, re-joins Alpha's squad waiting for him to go to *Deck A*, the Armoury. Captain Alpha looks away, pretending that he wasn't listening in on their conversation.

A jolly whistling greets them as they arrive at a long and narrow room, mostly empty except for a burly man with a black apron. He sits repairing a weapon, trying to solder two parts of a broken plasma rifle together. As they approach, he jumps out to attention, giving each an awkward salute as if he hasn't seen humans in a while. VanWest is a little taken aback by the man's crossed eyes, each one looking in the opposite direction. He can't but wonder how this man can do such delicate work with such vision.

The cross-eyed man is a little too quirky to be an Enforcer or, for that matter a member of the Universal Council, likely well adept at weaponry. 'Hey, folks! I'm Gunner, and my job is to get you boys kitted out for some bunker-busting entertainment. Excited'?

They salute him back as Gunner knocks on the wall twice, prompting the room to shift, the shelves jut out to reveal hundreds of weapons - an amazing armoury. There is a plethora of specialist equipment, from combat gear to long-range missiles and grenades.

VanWest is super impressed. These are some of the Universal Council's most advanced weapons. Many so secret that they are not even used in minor incursions or propaganda events, including the Universal Red and Blue Games, for fear that the NEA rebels could study them and learn how to counter their power.

The shelves are labelled:
Shelf 1. *Electroskeleton*. Device that fits over the hand to protect against and deflect plasma and laser shots.
Shelf 2 *Demron Uniforms*. Camouflage SWAT uniform: suit that blends into the immediate environment and cloaks one's body heat. Aquasuit: wetsuit equipped with O2Breather pockets.
Shelf 3. *Blasters*. Corner Shot: Three-direction gun made for bunker battles. Plasma blaster: used to disintegrate large

objects with its forceful plasma blast, penetrates forcefields, breaking down reinforced metal plated armour.

Shelf 4. *Range of Grenades*. Heat-seeking Electromagnetic Pulse grenades: deactivates shields and electrical gear. Flash grenades: stuns all nearby.

Shelf 5. *Computer Virus Uploads*. Trojan Virus: a computer virus that masks security systems including cameras, by repeating last known images. Resident Virus: Takes over implants and zombifies its host.

Shelf 6. *Camouflage Helmets*. Various protective headgear that adapt to different environments be it night-time raids, aqua dives, ice terrain, rocky terrain.

Shelf 7. *Upgrades and Trackers*. Weapon Augmenters. Taser amplifier: a stunner to add to heavy weapons. Surveillance tracker: a ball that maps the terrain ahead and scans for lifeforms. Special ops telescope: a thermal Moggle Spotter to discover hard to see enemies hiding far away.

Shelf 8. *Vibroweapons, Shields and Electrostaffs*. Laser sword, electro-scythe, lightning boomerang and reflector shield.

Shelf 9. *Missiles and Long-range Weapons*. Proton energy rifle: delivers a sharp pinpoint shot, range of up to two hundred miles. MajorLaser missile: A small but powerful projectile that can fix on to and hit targets thousands of miles away.

Shelf 10. *Ancillary Support*. Proton Net, Electrolock, Medical Kit, Food Capsules.

Gunner gets up and inspects the shelves, mumbling to himself, 'Bunker infiltration and travelling through water pipes, hmm, where are you'?

Dithering for a few moments, he grabs four aquasuits for the Enforcer squad from shelf 2, 'Ok boys! Gear up, take these O2Breather pills and get these outfits on. I'll grab you some bunker-busting weapons next'!

Gunner then moves over to the other shelves, picking out the Corner Shot rifles and a selection of bunker-busting grenades from shelves 3 and 4, which he puts into a crate. VanWest follows Gunner's instructions, most interested in the variety of weapons on *Shelf 8*. Especially that tagged *Electroskeleton*. He holds his right-hand close, the device, able to sense his presence, latches around his hand, stinging slightly as it attaches itself to his fingers' bones and wrist. Albeit a little sore, his whole hand feels strangely lighter as well as stronger.

Having taken the Corner Shot rifles and added some Surveillance trackers, Zheng and Dell are happy with Gunner's selection. They carry the crate to the transport elevator to get ready for the operation, changing into the aquasuits and taking the O2Breather pills. Alpha takes the Corner Shot and fixes on it a Taser amplifier, as well as an Electrolock, for he wants to be the one to capture Mad Newton and reap the rewards.

The Universal Council designated him the squad leader once again. Curiously, they always seem to put him in charge, always keen to champion him. Even though Alpha is a top athlete, everyone knows he's a hothead. His behaviour also not that of the Spartan way, that of an Enforcer, always putting himself ahead of others.

The whole team is ready to leave at sixteen hundred hours. Alongside their personally selected items they are transported into the loading bay, where a small arrowhead-shaped ship awaits them with the Colonel. The BoeingHawk special ops stealth glider is built for missions in highly populated zones. This craft gives a whole new meaning to superfast and stealthy, able to remain cloaked without making a sound as it travels at light speed. Its controls are second to none and with a skilled pilot, highly manoeuvrable even at top speed.

The craft transports the crate and squad inside the passenger hold, where the Colonel instructs the glider to commence take-off. The bay doors of the SCC-400 open, as soon as all have taken their seats the glider thrusts forward, flying through the streets towards the waterworks facility. Their operation to stop this 'New Beginning' and final leap begins.

Chapter 13 Back to the Cockroach Farm

It's a few minutes past four in the afternoon and being Autumn in Antarctica, the sun is already setting. The traffic is heavy from the citizens hurrying to make it home before dark and the treacherous night. This poses no issue for the BoeingHawk glider, which weaves through with ease, invisible to those it passes. There's now less than an hour to go until the estimated time of the leap.

The BoeingHawk reaches its destination within seconds, arriving at the operation's staging area at the top of the waterworks facility. It hovers over the four inverted cone-shaped water tanks, careful not to make a sound or cause any turbulence.

Phase 1 start - in the middle, a ladder leads to an entry point into the flood canal pipes and their path to the eel tank's access point - *Phase 2* infiltration of the surface level of the Utopian base - where the Trojan Virus should mask the security cameras.

The waterworks facility is eerily quiet, running at minimum capacity. Supporting Enforcer units have already taken up positions rounding up the waterworks' staff to minimise the risk of being spotted and the alarm being raised. Several cloaked units keep a short distance from the cockroach farm, ready to neutralise any Utopians that may try to get in or out.

Before disembarking the glider, the Colonel briefly recaps the tactical plan for the squad, the phases to begin once they reach the access point of the eel tank. It uploads to their Moggle Xs:

Phase 1: Descend from the waterworks facility, down the ladder and through the pipes to reach the electric eel tank's access point.

Phase 2: Wait for signal that the upload of the virus is complete, at, which point the timer will begin a countdown from 00:05:00. Captain Alpha and Captain VanWest to swim through to exit first and secure the passage to the furnace followed by Captains Dell and Zheng.

Phase 3: Captain Dell and Captain Zheng to infiltrate the bunker first through the black furnace, flames blast every 20 seconds. Alpha and VanWest to join once infiltration complete.

Phase 4: Proceed to level minus 3. Wait for the signal from our agent, codename T-I-T-O, before entering.

Phase 5: Dispatch all the Utopian targets, the other Enforcers will secure the top-level. Remember it is vital to bring back Mad Newton alive. Capture Alive!

The Colonel's role is akin to that of the Universal Red and Blue Games: he will stay in the glider to coordinate this complex operation. They ready themselves and set their Moggle X timers to five minutes. This will commence *Phase 2* entering the base on the Colonel's cue and once the agent has completed her upload of the Trojan Virus; causing the security system to show the previous images in a continuous loop for five minutes - the time required to get through the black furnace.

As they disembark, each removes their Corner Shot and grenades from the crate, slinging it across their backs. Captain Alpha and VanWest descend first, rappelling down. Upon landing, they place their plasma rifles forward and take point by the ladder. Captain Zheng and Dell rappel next and rush towards the water tank's ladder, sliding down it two rugs at the time to reach the access point to the pipes, the path to the cockroach farm and secret bunker base.

Alpha and VanWest join and keep guard as Zheng prises open the access panel enclosing the pipe's valve. Using a multi-tool, a silver square-shaped programming device, Zheng redirects the water's flow towards the farm and creates a pathway to the eel tank by opening up any other access valves along the way.

They wait until the Colonel sends the one-word signal, *'Enter'*.

Eager to take the lead, Alpha muscles to the front and enters into the pipe first. Being in charge of this mission, Alpha wants to impress and show himself to be Elite material, believing it best to look in command at all times. Despite knowing each other for quite a long-time, the relationship between VanWest and Alpha has never been warm, and since the Games even downright hostile. He seethes with jealousy at the prospect of VanWest becoming his superior.

Alpha hopes that this high-profile operation will earn him the same recognition. He's hungering to kill as many Utopians as possible and to be the one that captures Mad Newton. Winning thus his own ticket to Elite status. However, Alpha's eagerness immediately lands him into trouble. Stupidly he is caught off guard by the strong current and swept, nearly out of control, down the pipe in the direction of the cockroach farm. VanWest follows, more cautious about maintaining his balance, paddling to catch up, as do the others.

The current takes them straight to the first junction where a warning light signals that there are two routes ahead, on the left is the farm and eel tank. Alpha has managed to slow himself just enough to make the turn. The pipe is becoming much narrower, barely allowing them to fit through with their weapons. Fortunately, the current is weaker in this pipe, almost stagnant. And whilst the water level is much lower, the smell is more rancid, the water full of faeces.

As they wade through and reach the access point to the tank, a message from the Colonel rolls across their Moggle X lenses, flashing *T-Minus 00:05:00. Phase 2* infiltrating the bunker base is about to commence once the Trojan virus has uploaded.

A metallic mesh barrier covers the access point into the eel filled water tank. Keen to press on, Alpha slams the butt of his Corner Shot against it, breaking it open. At least wise enough not to discharge his weapon, as any heat signature could rile the eels and alert those inside. Several smaller eels are released through the opening and smack into Alpha's face, each emitting a mild electric shock, which is, luckily for him, absorbed by his aquasuit. Vexed, he reacts by violently smashing his rifle's butt against one who wriggles in the low and murky water until its long body is pounded into mush.

Opening the access point, the timer automatically blinks and vibrates, signalling them to enter the eel tank. They have *00:05:00* to get through the tank and the black furnace before the camera system returns to normal. Hopefully, the Utopians do not notice the loop made by the Trojan Virus. VanWest's mind wholly focused on the task of fulfilling Dr King's demands and following the Universal commandments; determined to capture Mad Newton and kill Iris.

Once again, Alpha enters first, with the rest following close behind. The tank's claw is motionless, the electric eels on their rest break, as planned, staying docile at the tank's bottom. They carefully swim across, so as to not get electrocuted or alert the Utopians. Any powerful jolt from the eel swarm would be fatal.

On the other side there is a ladder, their way out, close to the black furnace. Their cautious swim has slowed them down though, and upon Alpha reaching the ladder, the timer hits *00:03:30*. He jumps out without any consideration for his squad, splashing as he exits the water. Fortunately, for them, the eels are not skittish and remain placid.

Alpha jumps down into a pen filled with goo, cockroach excrement and fodder, and takes point to secure the path forward. VanWest follows next and does the same. Their aquasuits dry them instantly, Dell and Zheng take over as *Phase 3* commences. This is where their specialist skills will be most crucial to their success, infiltrating the black furnace and entering into the bunker.

The water in the eel tank has irritated VanWest eyes, he can't help but take a moment to rub them. Closing his eyes, he sees images. Flashes of Alpha knocking down Mad Newton before turning his rifle on Iris, who runs away. He re-opens his eyes to see an impatient Alpha signalling him to take up a position closer to the furnace. The timer is at *00:02:50*.

Up close, the black furnace is quite large and imposing. Several conveyor belts carry the cockroaches' gooey paste towards it, having scooped it up from the pens. The furnace's crankshafts gyrate up and down to mash it up further, emptying it inside the burner, whose flames sweep through every twenty seconds. Its heat boils the water in the tanks above to produce steam and charge the generator. One thing is for sure, there's no shortage of faeces here, along with the energy from the eel tank there's clearly enough to power a large base.

Standing back-to-back, VanWest and Alpha watch as their Moggle X timers pass *00:02:00*. Zheng and Dell are busy double-checking the furnace and its pattern of incineration, taking care to not get fried like the cockroach goo. They will also need to pass through with their specially adapted grenades and Corner Shots; to be used in *Phase 5* to eliminate any Utopian target who will likely take cover behind walls and blockades as they enter the site of their leap.

Zheng pulls down the first lever, timing it precisely as the flames cease, and squeezes inside, followed by Dell. Moving quickly to avoid incineration, Zheng reaches the second lever that opens up a hatch to the room behind, the bunker. Pulling it down, they both hurry through, well inside the allotted 20 seconds. Their preparedness has paid off. Dell and Zheng proceed to secure the room as they wait for Alpha and VanWest to join for *Phase 4*, hopefully unfried.

Alpha takes point once again, ordering Dell in an angry whisper to 'Move out of the way'.

VanWest glances at his timer, which feels like it has jumped forward - *00:00:58* - less than a minute remains! Alpha selfishly pulls him back, to ensure that he makes it through in time. Forcing VanWest to wait for a new sweep of flames to pass.

With barely 20 seconds remaining to get through before the Trojan virus expires, VanWest takes his one opportunity, squeezing through to reach *Phase 4* of the operation in the nick of time.

Alpha leads them down a spiral staircase, much worn with footprints, through three floors of disorientating turns until they reach the entrance of the third basement level. The Utopians are behind the reinforced metal door, they can even hear muffled voices inside. Dell looks up and notices, to his shock, that there is a security camera. This wasn't marked in the interface and operation planning!?

The intelligence didn't show this! What is more, there is no one to greet them, no agent. VanWest has been duped by the Seductress before, he fears she has double-crossed the Universal Council. It was all going a little too well.

Waaahhhh! Before he can say anything, a siren sounds, its sharp noise jarring inside their ears and causing them to stumble back. Ignoring a message coming through from the Colonel, *Phase 4 Compromised, Proceed With Caution to Phase 5*, Alpha reacts without and charges the door, breaking it open with a single kick.

Zheng and Dell unable to stop him, have no other option but to follow in. Commencing their infamous ZhengDell technique of attack, they fire their Corner Shots in quick succession, the plasma whizzing around to find targets.

However, it is Zheng that is met first by a shot, striking him straight - *boom* - in the forehead, scattering his brain tissue gruesomely over VanWest's face. Stunned, VanWest sees a flash of the Seductress leaping and then Iris. Then another flash this time of the charred and twisted wreck of *ENDEA* on the white sand. He knows the Utopians are commencing the leap.

Boom-boom! An enraged Dell immediately counters, firing his Corner Shot again into the darkened room. Alpha manages to dodge the Utopian countermeasures as he charges in, throwing an electromagnetic grenade as he does so. This time Dell's Corner Shot finds its targets, as they bounce across the walls, hitting several Utopians in quick succession. VanWest races through to take up a position behind a large concrete pillar, covering for Dell and Alpha as they push forward. Their Moggle X lenses helping them to identify and neutralise their targets.

The firefight illuminates the whole room, revealing Mad Newton, the Seductress and Iris all crowded together in the far corner. It looks like the Utopians are doing their best to slow their progress, sacrificing themselves to keep them away from the trio. Allowing them to leap!

The third commandment plays in his mind, *to destroy all those who defy the Universal Council*. It has now been over 47 hours since VanWest has returned to the Year 3000 from 1951 Paris. A period of time that has included: fighting giant cockroaches; escaping a powerplant; meeting and learning about Iris and her father, finding out more about his own past and then subsequently being tortured on the accusation of abetting them; and now this!

With Alpha and Dell neutralising their targets in quick succession, VanWest moves to capture Mad Newton. However, he feels a familiar cold whistle, a wind pulling at him, as he approaches. The same feeling as in the cellar, also before his leap to the city of light. The Utopian's 'New Beginning' having commenced.

Boom-Boom! Alpha reaches Mad Newton first, he swings around the pillar and fires a series of Taser amplifier shots towards him. Whilst most of the shots whizz around, pulled away by the portal, one of the shots manages to find its target, hitting Mad Newton and sending him into a spasm. VanWest readies to shoot at Iris, but something stops him from discharging his rifle, he cannot fire it. He cannot kill her.

The Seductress is closest to the portal. She leaps inside as Alpha slides into Mad Newton, securing his prize, his winning ticket to what he hopes will be Elite status. And, as VanWest foresaw earlier, he next turns his rifle on Iris. She edges closer to the portal, unsure whether to try and save her father or run. Seeing Alpha line up another shot, she is left with no other choice than to turn and leap before it can reach her. The firefight ceases as Dell discharges a 3-shot blast that pulverises the last set of Utopians resisting them.

A furious Alpha throws an Electrolock on an incapacitated Mad Newton before storming over and grabbing VanWest by his throat. With the portal closing, he lifts him up from the floor, 'You roachtard, you better go get her, or you will have a date with my blaster. You are not going cost me my promotion. Follow'!

Releasing him, he throws him towards the portal. Remembering Dr King's instruction to 'follow', he dives headfirst in with a last parting message from Alpha calling him a 'Roachtard'!

Spiralling through the vortex, he knows not where he will arrive in the past but if he doesn't find and stop the Utopians that leapt, time in the present as he knows it will be altered. It could even be that the Universal Council, as well as his own existence, never comes to pass. His mind is conflicted with that of his heart. He could not bring himself to kill Iris, breaking with it his commandment to destroy all those who defy the Universal Council.

VanWest asks himself, what is this feeling?

Chapter 14   Leap to Utopia

Splash! VanWest enters into a pool of water. Lucky to be in his Enforcer aquasuit, he finds himself surrounded by strange red and green plants, and roots of what must be trees, standing stilt-like from further below. A bright light shines, drawing him in, but as he swims across several bubbles pass him by and he catches sight of a small shiny object drifting along.

He recognises the object, a silver necklace, snapped in half, it looks just like the one resting on the bosom of the Seductress, back in 1951 Paris. Diving deeper towards the light, his eyes widen in horror, finding that it originates from a rifle still attached to a severed hand!

Drifting close by is the rest of the man, his face blanched and his pupils dilated, his body limp and lifeless - a small *U* behind his ear identifying him as a Utopian. Strangely, this man hasn't been killed by one of the squad's plasma blasts or grenades but by a blade - his hand severed his throat cut. The blood still seeping, the kill fresh.

Matching his face to the *Most Wanted*, it confirms him to be a very high-profile Utopian: Ankit Bhargav 'The Priest'. He must have leapt before the squad stormed the room. Being one of the most devout, he was a perfect choice for Mad Newton's mission, their leap to this 'New Beginning'. VanWest is puzzled, with the Seductress's snapped necklace close by he wonders if she has met the same fate. But there is no other body.

A Moggleapp tablet protrudes out of the Priest's metallic grey backpack. On its screen, VanWest can make out four large letters spelling *NASA*. As he removes the man's bag from the dead body, he spots in the corner of his eye a large shadow gliding along.

Suddenly something scaly brushes against his leg and nudges him forward. A second nudge soon follows from the other side, knocking his plasma rifle out of his hand. The light from the Priest's rifle revealing a creature with a long snout packed with sharp jagged teeth and scaly skin.

VanWest turns, only to find its narrow yellow eyes glaring back at him. Three more of its ilk appear, gliding along the bottom, they encircle the cadaver of the Priest, acting as if a wild pack of dogs protecting their meal from an unwelcome stranger. VanWest has heard of these creatures, they are alligators, and thus knows to back away. Their reputation as deadly killers is well-documented in the Universal Council's Wiki.

Despite these prehistoric cold-blooded reptiles surviving many millions of years, outliving thousands of species and many disasters, they could not survive man, noted extinct near to the end of the third millennium. In the end, only surviving in labs in order to provide the Elites with an exotic food, that is until they lost interest. Nevertheless, rumours persist that some still survive in remote Equatorial Earth. Marooned inside the shallow lakes of dormant volcanoes of the Central Americas where the water is still relatively low in radioactive particles. Lands that humans no longer visit.

VanWest panics, he uses his Electroskeleton hand to emit a shockwave pulse that pushes them away and him up to the water's surface. Hastily he swims to the shore and climbs out the water onto an elevated section of mangrove. His heart pounding and head still dizzy from the leap through the portal, he takes a moment to catch his breath. This place, this 'New Beginning', is covered in subtropical plant life. Nothing like this exists in the year 3000, so very green. Despite these alligators, this place does look Utopian-like.

The air, whilst clean like that of 1951 Paris, is sticky hot. It starts to rain and the wind is picking up. Happy that it isn't acidic, he knows he still needs to move on before the weather worsens.

His Quantum Communicator implant activates, 'Come in… VanWest, come in! Do you copy'?

'Affirmative, copy that... Commissioner Ming'? He responds, still catching his breath.

Commissioner Ming asks, 'Report on situation'?

'Situation critical. Landed in swamp with strange creatures. One hostile dead, Utopian called the Priest. Cannot confirm why dead'.

'Captain VanWest, be sure, our intelligence tells us the location of their leap is Everglades, State of Florida, in late 1990s United States. Transmitting Wiki supplements'.

Wiki Download
The Everglades are a natural region of subtropical wetlands in the southern portion of the US state of Florida, comprising of a large watershed in its southern half. The system begins near Orlando with the Kissimmee River, which discharges into the shallow Lake Okeechobee. The wetlands are comprised of harmless vegetation that includes green sawgrass, tropical hardwood hammocks and pines. Home to several deadly creatures. Over 8ft long alligators and snakes. Stay out of the water!

VanWest finds it hard to focus on his Quantum Communicator and to talk longer, 'Affirmative, received. Commissioner... will report once establish area is safe. Remaining alert for hostiles'.

'Wait'! Dr King joins the communication, 'Lest I must say, do not hesitate to kill her. Do not hesitate'!

'My liege, affirmative. One question if I may'? VanWest asks.

'Go ahead'.

'The Seductress'?

'Kill her too! This woman is now on no one's side but her own. Lest I must say, this deviant, devious creature wants this leap for her own selfish gain'! Dr King warns.

The Seductress played them all, she was meant to be the Universal Council's agent inside the bunker. She double-crossed them, as she did with the Utopians, delaying the squad's entry into the third basement level. This seems to have been all a well-timed ruse that saw the majority of the Utopians killed and Mad Newton captured. Allowing herself enough time to leap to 1998 Florida. Her plan clear: to make this final leap alone with the only working Quantum Accelerator rod.

With Ankit Bhargav 'The Priest' killed, it seems only Iris, herself and VanWest are left in this 'New Beginning' with no other dead body around to confirm otherwise.

Commissioner Ming adds in an ominous voice, before ending the communication, 'Remember VanWest, be sure the Universal is all-knowing. Remember the commandments and your mission. Do not fail us'!

The Wiki supplement is not the only thing that has been transmitted through time. VanWest can feel his mind tingle and narrow, the Universal Council's three commandments transfixing his thoughts, commanding him to kill both women. They take over his will, filling his head with 'ideas not of his own'.

Pulling out the Priest's tablet, he interfaces with it and finds an entry titled *Endeavour STS 88*. Crosschecking its name with his Wiki, it returns with some interesting information:

Endeavour... transmitting... STS 88, space shuttle launched December 4, 1998, from Kennedy Centre, Merritt Island, Florida. With the second section of the ISS, Unity Node. Construction of the International Space Station began on November 20, 1998, when the American-funded, Russian-built Zarya module, was launched into the orbit around Earth. Sixteen countries were involved in the project. The Unity Node - with one stowage rack and two pressurised adapters attached - was a docking hub used to join sections of the space station together. Major construction of the ISS started when Endeavour's astronauts locked Zarya and Unity together. The US laboratory Destiny was added in 2001, followed by the European Columbus and Japanese Kibo labs in 2008. Humongous in size, the ISS took 13 years to complete at a cost equal to the yearly GDP of a wealthy nation.

He searches for more entries and finds several photos of interest, one tagged *Everglades Homestead, December 2, 1998,* looks very similar to where he has arrived. Other photos are tagged with the names of astronauts and the final photo, tagged *Cape Kennedy Mission Control, Merritt Island,* is of a control room filled with rows of widescreen monitors. The date of this final photo is *December 4, 1998.* It looks like this Cape Kennedy is the Utopian's first target.

Continuing his search, he finds a very familiar sounding tag, *The New Beginning.* The same Mad Newton used when inviting him to join his Utopian mission. He reads through the text:

Our mission is to rid the world of harmful technologies. Hans Ashtar taught us machines would influence the way we behave and that we must resist these machines' external pressure on our moral decision-making. As Utopians, these are our five commandments.

The Utopian Five Commandments:
Commandment 1. Treat all post 20th-century technology as evil.
Commandment 2. Protect planet Earth, and work to restore it to full health, including its creatures, the forests, grasslands, seas and lakes.
Commandment 3. No man, woman or child shall consume more than is needed. All resources must be evenly spread amongst Earth's people.
Commandment 4. Only recognise life-forms as those created by God. It is forbidden for man to forge and create new life-forms. This includes A.I. and cyborgs.
Commandment 5. DO NOT serve the Universal Council and any other unelected authority. Only work with non-Utopians in order to defeat them.

The New Beginning:

The Utopians will transcend time and return it back to December 1998, infiltrate the highest echelons and obtain positions of influence and power

These are the following world and technological events to target if comes to pass:

1998 – Launch of Unity Node, connecting Russian & US parts of the ISS Station

1998 – Building of CERN's Large Hadron Collider, particle accelerator starts

2001 – US laboratory Destiny attached to ISS station

2002 – Founding of SpaceX by Elon Musk, focused on building Mars settlement

2003 – China becomes 3rd nation to launch a human into orbit

2004 – Mike Mervill flies 1st private vehicle, SpaceShipOne, to the edge of space

2005 – Launch of Google web mapping service

2005 – Mars Reconnaissance Orbiter, maps 99% of Mars and finds meltwater

2008 – Scientists reprogram skin cells into stem cells, without use of embryos

2008 – Scientists figure out how to regrow human organs from stem cells

2008 – Inaugural test of CERN's Large Hadron Collider particle accelerator

2011 – China launches 1st space lab, Tiangong, 1st step to manned space station

2013 – Election of Chinese Premier, pro-space development

2017 – Election of US President, pro-space development

2019 – US President launches a new armed service, the Space Force

2020 – NASA first private astronauts go to space for a relatively low price

The scale of Mad Newton's mission is much more extensive than VanWest first thought. The bombing of the UNESCO meeting to kill Francois de Rose in 1951 Paris may have even been a decoy or a practice run to set up this 'New Beginning'.

The launch to attach the Unity Node to ISS is the first in a timeline of targets that stretches right up to 2020. A shrewd move, given the leap commenced a little earlier than 48 hours. In the scenario, the Utopians didn't arrive at the correct date and place, there were further events that they could disrupt to slow and stop scientific and technological advancement. The timeline also shows another concern, the progress on stem cell science during this era, linked to the immortal Elites, humans living much longer than normal. Able to rule for far too long.

VanWest tips out the contents of the Priest's backpack, hoping to find more clues about the mission. It contains a handheld temporal facial re-modulation kit, several identity cards, and a printed metallic sheet with twenty codenames along with geocodes. The codenames likely those of the other Utopians that should have leapt for this mission. If it were not for the Seductress's betrayal, then they would be here too, in the past.

It is not entirely clear what the Seductress actually seeks, now a renegade armed not only with 30th-century technology but also with knowledge of this location and era's history. Could it be she wants to manipulate it for her own benefit? Maybe she seeks to make herself the ruler of this world, just like the Council does hundreds of years later. If Iris is alive, she may be unaware of her betrayal. With the Priest dead she is now the only true Utopian left to carry out this 'New Beginning'.

The creation of CERN, the building of ISS was not just a major step forward in science but also in International co-operation. It was key in the commencement of long-distance space travel and a space race between Earth's superpowers of the time, USA and China. These nations sought power and prestige as well as resources, destroying Earth and forcing the ancestors of the 'citizens' to flee from their homes and once habitable lands.

VanWest deducts that if Iris is trying to stop the launch of the ISS' second module, then she must be heading to Merritt Island, Cape Kennedy - the place where the Unity node is launched. Like with the bombing of the UNESCO meeting and implication of the Swiss delegates, the plot must be something that creates serious discord and stops progress for decades to come.

His mind focuses on the launch itself, what exactly is Iris's plot? Creating a problem between the US and Russia, the builders of the first ISS module Zarya would be a likely objective. An act of sabotage that results in the death of the Russian astronaut onboard would ignite a major row between the partners. By itself, the deaths of astronauts are well-documented in the Universal Council's Wiki as a major reason for the slow evolvement of space travel at its beginning. Indeed, many safety measures stem from this era with questions over risk versus reward. If this were to happen to ISS at such an early and critical stage, then progress could be halted for not only decades but also for centuries.

With no ISS, China's ambitions may slow too and a space race may never happen. Well, at least not at the scale of that in the 21st and 22nd century. ISS' pivotal work would also be lost, including insights on how humankind could survive in space; the effect of zero gravity on the human body; how to grow crops in space; and the testing of new spacecraft systems and equipment required for future missions to the Moon and Mars. SpaceX, the world's first private space travel company, would never be created, its first mission to send a cargo load to the ISS in 2012.

The silver Quantum Accelerator rod is not in the bag, he needs to find the women, not just to kill them, for without it he will be stuck in the past!

Revisiting the first photo he found, tagged *Everglades Homestead*, he recognises that there is a mooring with three strange-looking crafts. VanWest zooms in, his Wiki returning: *Fan boats, flat-bottomed vessels propelled by an aircraft engine, allowing the driver to glide over and navigate low-lying water.*

Using his Moggle X, he scans it again, hoping to locate a route to this location. Analysing the fan boats, the terrain and the fauna in the photo, it returns a match, VanWest turns around and finds the boats were behind him all along. However, there is one difference - only two fan boats are moored. The Seductress and or Iris must have taken one. The rain picking up, VanWest plods through the mangrove. Close by there is a wooden directional post, *Homestead General Aviation Airport, 5 Miles.*

VanWest can see no other body, alive or dead, in the vicinity, he can only assume that they are still together going to the locations on the tagged photos. This makes sense, Iris leapt last, allowing the Seductress time to kill the Priest before her arrival.

His Moggle X and Wiki show that the quickest route to Cape Kennedy is flying from Homestead Airport to the Space Coast Regional Airport, approximate journey time of *01:00:00*. With the rain turning into a torrential downpour; it's not going to be easy to fly a plane and even to get to the airport. It's surely going to be a very bumpy ride.

As he hurries to the closest fan boat, the crackling of leaves and dead wood under his feet, combined with the rain, draw up several familiar yellow eyes to the water's surface. Having acquired a penchant for human flesh after devouring the Priest, the alligators stalk him. Luckily for him, the fan boat has a key in the ignition. His Wiki contains instructions on how to use it, taking the high seat he twists the key, powering up the propeller and causing its huge fan to rotate - *roar.*

Pulling the large lever stick to his left side, the boat jolts forward its force so strong it catches him by surprise. He does well to stay seated. Fortunately, the controls are a little more straightforward than that of the car in 1951 Paris, closer to the joystick controls of a hovercar. He quickly masters its mechanics, turning the stick to steer in the right direction. The craft moves most unusually, skipping over the water, it swings to the now frequent heavy wind gusts that sweep through.

Making haste towards Homestead, weaving through the sawgrass, he can see a faint light shining through the heavy rain and wind. His mind is filled with thoughts not his own; stuck in a paradox, an overwhelming need to kill Iris, only for his heart to object, desperately wanting to save her, that is if she is even still alive. All it can agree on is finding her fast.

The light grows brighter as he progresses, and with the help of his Moggle X, he can see it comes from behind a rusty shack perched over the water. It has a mooring. As he nears a deafening - *roar* - diverts his attention, he looks up and finds a small craft lifting off into the air. His Wiki identifies it as a *Small High-winged, Single-piston Engine Cessna Plane*. It is a plane taking off, this must be the airport! Behind the shack is a mile-long strip of yellow lights, a landing strip.

VanWest slows, securing the boat to the mooring before jumping onto its floating jetty. He does well to keep his balance with the heavy rain and wind causing it to swing side to side. Keen to make up time, he hurries to this landing strip, passing a sign that reads *Homestead General Aviation Airport*, confirming he has indeed reached his target destination. His Moggle X zooms in on a large hollow building close by, a hangar. With the heavy wind, no other plane taxis for take-off.

Heading inside the hangar, he finds another Cessna plane. This could be his best bet for getting to Merritt Island and Cape Kennedy. However, he is forced to duck and hide behind some crates as a short fat man wearing shorts and a flowery shirt appears. He is inspecting it, ticking off what appears to be a checklist on a clipboard. VanWest waits for the man to leave before re-emerging, thinking it best to avoid any contact that could alter the time continuum. With no one now around, VanWest jumps onto the plane's wing and, forgetting his own strength, nearly yanks the pilot's door straight off its hinges.

Several archaic items are inside; a map, a compass, a leather black bomber jacket, a flare gun and several bars of something that he has never seen before labelled *MILK CHOCOLATE*. Hungry and figuring them to be food, he tears off its brown wrapper and takes a bite; it's very yummy and before he knows it has devoured them all in quick succession. Chocolate doesn't exist in the year 3000, at least not in this form, it tastes so sweet.

But before he can take the pilot seat a low-pitched voice calls out to him, 'Hey there, Mister'!

A startled VanWest turns to find that the short fat man with the flowery shirt has returned.

'What you doing on my plane, Mister'? The man asks, nervously edging backwards to what appears to be a red pull lever behind a glass panel, an alarm! He is staring at VanWest's strange third millennia Enforcer aquasuit like he has just seen an alien.

Acting fast, VanWest grabs the flare gun and aims it straight at the man's head, 'Freeze'! Causing the pilot to stumble and fall backwards.

Seeing the man's confused and frightened reaction to his appearance, he knows he needs to change and orders the man to undress, 'Shirt, shorts, shoes'!

The man promptly complies, throwing his clothes towards VanWest. He knows he can't let this man remember what has happened: his aquasuit, his threat, his person all could affect the time continuum. Using Master Jiang's technique, he walks calmly over to the man and delivers a swift, sharp jab just above his right ear, close to the medial temporal lobe, the part of the brain that houses short-term memory. The man should be knocked out for a few hours and not remember a thing.

After dragging the unconscious man behind some boxes, he changes into his clothes then climbs back up and into the pilot's seat. He uses his Moggle X's recommended flight path to the Space Coast Regional Airport and checks his Wiki for instructions on how to take-off and fly this primitive craft, this Cessna plane.

VanWest takes the control stick and fires up the engine, which propels the plane forward. He guides the plane out of the hangar and lines it up on the runway, mindful to keep his lights off and not attract attention. It's not too indifferent to a HyperSphere simulation, something he has practised once or twice. Luckily, the heavy rain and wind mask its noise, allowing him to successfully elude the control tower. Pulling the control stick back, he accelerates down the runway till the plane lifts into the blustery air, pushing him back against the seat. He's taking off!

Chapter 15   A Killer's Love

The streetlights shine brightly in the dark as he struggles to fly through the heavy wind and rain, a little shocked at how this craft shakes so much, such a contrast to the Enforcer patrol ships, which remain perfectly stable in any weather. After close to an hour, the Space Coast Regional Airport is in view. The lights of its landing strip are brighter than those of the Homestead, and its tarmac stretches much further.

He checks his Wiki for instructions on how to land, which recommends to radio into the control tower first, *To Secure Clear Landing Path*. Though it is risky to alert them to his plane, he doesn't want to collide with another. Making use of its primitive transponder, he picks up the headset that is attached by a coiled cable, putting it over his ears. Using the recommended flight phonetics of the time, he speaks, 'Must land, Mike Uniform Sierra Tango Lima Alpha November Delta'.

'Copy that, runway clear, Yankee Echo Sierra, you are good to land', the flight controller confirms.

VanWest aligns his plane in between the lights of the runway and pushes the control stick forward to start the descent, the turbulence causing the plane and his stomach to bounce around. Managing to remain calm, he descends, doing well to stay in a straight line and soon hits the runway with a loud *thump*! The slippery landing strip makes for a nervy finish, forcing him to pull the stick all the way back in order to slow down. Fortunate to not skid off the tarmac, he comes to a stop.

He steers the plane towards those parked close by, spotting a Cessna plane with *Homestead* painted in red letters on its side. It's exactly like the one that he saw taking off whilst on the fan boat and matching to his Moggle X records. He opens the plane's door, this time remembering to take care and armed only with his Electroskeleton hand proceeds to this plane. The still blustery wind and rain drench his baggy cotton shorts and shirt and he starts to shiver. Apart from the cockpit door being left open nothing looks unusual, all he can see is a couple of empty cans with *SODA written on it*.

As he leans further in he notices two grey Demron jumpsuits tucked under the passenger seat, Hubert's brand didn't exist in this time!? The women must have been on this plane! He surveys the landing strip once again using his bionic sensors and his Moggle X for better visuals, it returns with *No Females In Close Proximity*.

All he can detect is an odd low humming noise, it belongs to a vehicle whose headlights now shine towards his plane. Written on the vehicle's bonnet are the words *Space Regional Airport Security*. Startled, he realises he has only a few moments to disguise himself. He does not want to resort to Master Jiang's technique of inflicting short-term memory loss again. He hurries back to his plane, jumping onto its wing and then into the cockpit.

Racking his brain for a plausible backstory, he rummages through the Priest's backpack and finds an ID belonging to a NASA Engineer on Endeavour, Flight STS 88, *D. Drake, born San Jose, California*. This could work well. He pulls out the facial re-modulation kit next and calibrates it to match that of the ID. Just about managing to complete the alteration to his facial features; turning his hair colour black, with only his eyes now looking his own before the vehicle pulls up.

A guard, wearing a badge and gun, gets out and saunters over to his plane, with a smile, he calls out, 'Hey there, Mister! Sure is raining like a cow pissing on a flat rock here. Ya fly in this'?

VanWest simply nods in response, not entirely sure what he's saying. The guard speaks English, but his accent is even heavier than that of the pilot he knocked out in Homestead. His Moggle X and Wiki identifies it as a Southern drawl, typical of the southern states during this century.

'Mister, ya have some ID'? The security man asks.

VanWest duly complies, climbing down from the plane's wing to hand him the ID card of the engineer he now looks like, *D. Drake*. Keeping a firm eye on the guard's holstered and primitive-looking gun.

'Golly, ya work for NASA!? Ya looking pretty soaked, must be colder than a witch's tit in a brass bra! I'll give ya a ride', the guard offers, with a friendly chuckle.

'Sure, thanks'! VanWest smiles, worried about leaving the Demron jumpsuits in the other plane, but he has no option. He doesn't want to look suspicious by walking over to the other plane and not accepting the ride. Thus, he takes only the items inside the Priest's backpack and walks with him over, stepping into the front passenger seat.

A little star-struck, the guard gives him a salute, 'By the way, my name is Wyatt. I'll sort ya out with a rental car, take ya to Space Kennedy. Ok'?

'Yeah sure, Wyatt'! VanWest replies, trying to mimic his disguise, with a light Californian twang. Keen to find the women, he inquires, 'Seen two ladies landing recently'?

'Sure did, they come from the plane right there - pretty little blond and a frizzy-haired lady. Ya know them? They said they were part of NASA too', Wyatt answers with a big smile, revealing that the women have yet to alter their appearance.

'Sure... We were going to meet at the airport but hey the weather'! VanWest answers.

'Women for ya! Say one thang and do another. They heading to an apartment near the NASA Causeway'. The security guard, Wyatt, continues, remarking on the women's looks, again chuckling, 'If ya don't mind me saying, dang! Those women weren't hit with no ugly stick. Never met two women look so fine, not in this Sunshine State, yer NASA boys sure pick them good - *OoooweeE*'!

VanWest gives a wry smile, he needs more details on where they went, 'Sure are... an apartment you said'?

'They're bickering about some Montgomery House, on Horizon drive or something. Know it'?

Crackle! The guard's walkie-talkie interrupts their conversation; it's a warning, 'Watch out! Plane-hijacking Homestead! Stand-by for more details, over and out'.

Wyatt looks at VanWest, 'Sir, I must ask, where ya flying in from today'?

'M-Miami! That's hella sketchy'! VanWest replies, hesitating before thinking of the name of a major city in Florida, at the same time doing his best to act surprised. It seems that the pilot has been found and his missing plane called in.

'These parts are sure getting more dangerous. All those illegals, with their narcotics in their britches'. VanWest nods, not sure what he means.

Wyatt looks keen to go and search the airport, 'Sir, it been a real pleasure, I got to skedaddle, Jolene fix ya up with a rental'.

The security vehicle stops in front of a single-storey building, ARRIVALS, he shouts through the door, 'Hey Jolene'!

A rather rotund woman shouts back, 'What ya want'?

Wyatt replies, 'Car for this NASA fella'!

VanWest steps out and gives a salute to Wyatt, who returns a second with an even bigger smile. Inside, Jolene asks for his details, pointing over at a parked car, 'It that red number, right over there. Give me some ID, I'll charge it to our NASA visitor account'.

The rental car is a red Nissan Maxima, a popular and cheap car model of the late 1990s. Jolene tries to strike up a conversation, 'Ya hear someone steal a plane in this wind. Crazy hey! Must have been as drunk as a skunk'!

VanWest gives a nervous smile back, for unbeknownst to her, he's the man who stole it, and no, he is not drunk like a skunk! Whatever that means.

She adds, 'Only manual left. All hunky-dory for ya?

'Sure, thanks'!

He thinks best not to mention that the last car he drove in manual likely still rests at the bottom of the river Seine, Paris. With his mind focused on finding the women, he's not keen to chit-chat and takes the keys. Hurrying to the parked car, he figures how to unlock by pressing a button on the key chain and steps inside.

Vroom! The engine ignites and he pulls out - *screech* - onto the driveway. Before steering onto the main road, he stops briefly to find the route with his Moggle X, returning with the direction to *Horizon Drive*. As he drives, the rain starts to ease and the sun slowly rises. Speeding down the highway, he can't but help notice this wondrous and strange world around him. More and more seeing why this time and place could be viewed as Utopian.

There is greenery everywhere, the highway is lined with grass, scrubs and tall palm trees. Soaring high above in the blue skies are birds of multiple colours. VanWest opens his window, allowing the wind to blow across his face. It's a sensation that cannot be found in any Hypersphere simulation, the air so fresh, clean and crisp. Further behind the trees is an azure-blue ocean. It is not incarnadine, like in the year 3000, but actually blue! The sun's light-refracting a multitude of colours off its ripples. However, his mind has drifted further from his control, in particular, one commandment plays in his head, to destroy all those who defy the Universal Council.

Passing by a sign, *Space Kennedy Visitor Complex 12 Miles*, his Moggle X indicates that *Horizon Drive* is very close. VanWest tries to anticipate the Seductress's next move, likely biding her time to kill Iris in the apartment, perhaps waiting for her to fall asleep. She poses the greatest risk of the two, a wildcard. Unlike Iris and her Utopian mission; there are no clues to her plans, as well as possible destinations of any future leap. Having manipulated this leap to her own selfish gain; she appears to only want this world for herself.

He focuses on his Quantum Communicator and sends through a message to Commissioner Ming with his updated status, 'In pursuit, closing in on target'.

The response is almost instant, 'Kill Iris. Kill Seductress'. The words latch onto his mind as he mutters the same words hypnotically out loud to himself, 'Kill Iris. Kill Seductress. Kill Iris. Kill Seductress'.

VanWest turns into Horizon Drive, sitting low in his car's seat as he surveys the buildings, doing his best not to be seen. Looking left and right, he soon locates Montgomery house, a yellow art-deco, four-storey high apartment block. Fortunately, it's still early, the street is quiet. He parks his car a short distance away and walks cautiously up the sidewalk, trying not to make any noise. Taking a moment to tweak his bionic sensors in order to pick-up any signs that may identify them.

On the ground floor, there is nothing that indicates the women are here. Continuing to the back, he finds an external concrete staircase with the gate unlocked. Remaining alert, he walks up to the next floor and steps onto a large terrace that stretches across two apartments. The Commissioner's last instruction, still playing like a broken record in the back of his mind, *Kill Iris. Kill Seductress'*.

His bionics now detect matching signatures of two human women and there's a curious low grumbling sound - *mmm* - as if one has been muffled. Tiptoeing towards the window of the apartment, careful not to alert anyone within to his presence, he picks up even more human sounds of distress, including a fastening heartbeat and the grinding of teeth.

Before he can peer through the window to confirm it is them, the door handle twists - *squeak*, forcing himself to step back, pressing his body against the wall. He was too loud, a circular-shaped silver proton gun protrudes out, held tightly by a slender female hand. Knowing he must react, he doesn't hesitate, grabbing hold of the woman's wrist and forcefully slamming it against the doorframe, throwing the gun to the floor. It's the Seductress. Belying her slender and slight appearance is a trained fighter who returns a sharp kick to his ribs - *crack* - and then throws him down with a well-executed judo Naga-Waza move - *thump*.

From the floor, he catches sight of a bound and gagged Iris. She mumbles - *mmm*. The Seductress does a forward roll and retrieves her proton gun. VanWest though reacts faster, using his Electroskeleton hand, he sends a shockwave - *whoosh* - that throws her into the railing, smashing the proton gun. The Seductress, realising the jig is up, unable to match this well-armed and trained Enforcer, leaps off the terrace with catlike agility.

Hitting the ground feet first, she disappears into the shadows. Spotting the silver Quantum Accelerator rod on the table beside Iris, VanWest decides its best to secure it first and to kill Iris before giving chase. The Seductress now less of a risk.

A seated and bound Iris stares at him, her wrists tied to the arms of a chair. VanWest's mind still plays the same words over and over, *Kill Iris. Kill Seductress.* His hand trembles as he grabs a knife from the kitchen counter and points it towards her slender neck. He cannot disobey, he must follow the commandments of the Universal Council:

1. To serve without question the Universal Council
2. To work for the progression of man and the Universal
3. To destroy all those who defy the Universal Council

His mind and heart are conflicted, he does not know who or what to listen to. Moving the knife closer to Iris's slender neck, he cannot help but notice her mesmerising electric blue eyes. She stares at him, hers filled with despair but also full of love. The same childlike look that she gave when kissing him under the stairs before the matron took her away. A solitary tear rolls down her cheek as VanWest struggles for control. With one hand he pulls the rag from her mouth, only for the other to press the knife against her neck, causing a drop of blood to trickle down.

'My love... I love you'! She repeats to him.

'You love me'? VanWest mutters back, still holding the knife firmly against her neck. No one has ever told him that they love him.

'I do, my love! The Council are evil, do not listen to them, block them out. Defy them, I plead with you'!

A sharp pain pierces through his head, dropping him onto his knees. His mind in flux, he thrusts the knife down into the chair's arm, narrowly missing Iris's wrist. The battle between his mind and heart overwhelming him. The commandments and message to 'Kill' now replaced by a vision of a place he has seen before; of him in an arena, the floor underneath covered with sand. His name being chanted, 'VanWest'.

With her restraints cut loose against the knife's blade, stuck in the chair's arm, Iris cradles him gently. His head on her lap, she repeats softly, 'I love you'.

Across them is a mirror. No longer does he look like the Californian Engineer D. Drake. Staring back is a dishevelled and exhausted version of himself, his eyes bloodshot and skin pale. They start to close.

VanWest has seen this arena before but not so vividly. This time Alpha is laughing loudly as he stands triumphantly over the limp and lifeless body of Iris. Attempting to shout at her, he finds himself to be mute, left helplessly to watch as her blood slowly runs towards him, slithering through the sand as if it were a dark red snake in the desert. Above is Dr King nodding in approval, wearing the same toga and gold-leafed corona as in the Universal Red and Blue Games, his right fist clenched tightly and raised triumphantly towards the sky.

Chapter 16   The Past

VanWest wakes up in a bed, his body naked and the sun now setting. Looking across, he finds that Iris is not there. Calling out her name 'Iris', there is no reply.

He searches for the silver Quantum Accelerator rod that he saw before on the table, but it is too nowhere to be found. He wonders how Iris could have left without waking him first. Maybe she couldn't wake him, him being so out of it. His baggy shorts and flowery shirt, those of the pilot from Homestead, lay neatly folded at the end of the bed. And, on the breakfast counter, he finds a paper with *the words of Emily Dickinson, a female poet from the 19th century:*

> *Success is counted sweetest*
> *By those who ne'er succeed.*
> *To comprehend a nectar*
> *Requires sorest need.*
> *Not one of all the purple Host*
> *Who took the Flag today*
> *Can tell the definition*
> *So clear of victory*
> *As he defeated – dying –*
> *On whose forbidden ear*
> *The distant strains of triumph*
> *Burst agonized and clear!*

Could it explain why she has left, is it her fear of failure? Her failure to complete her Utopian mission? He turns the page on the notepad to find not a poem but rather an instruction.

My Love,
Play the green chip. You will then understand the sacrifice I must make.
Your sweet, Iris X.
P.S. Try the Popping Tarts.

VanWest moves his hand behind his ear and feels a tingling sensation. He had completely forgotten about the green hexagon chip he was given by Mad Newton. Amazingly, it has managed to survive his interrogation onboard the SCC-400. It must have been well disguised, the NEA-Utopians so skilled at espionage and hacking. Activating it, the chip jars, sending a high-pitched whistle through his mind. It interfaces with his cerebral cortex, which in turn stimulates his hippocampus, the place in the brain where long-term memory is stored.

Long forgotten memories flood back. The first takes him back to the year 2980, his birth year, where he lies in a crib swaddled in a foil blanket, gazing at a hanging star and planet, which slowly rotates clockwise. The crib stands in a dimly lit room alongside two neighbouring cribs, though both are empty. Each has been marked with a red cross, and four large letters, *T-E-S-T*. His own crib bears no red cross. Instead, it has a name, *Van der Westhuizen A1*.

Pacing nervously in front is a woman dressed in a white lab coat, she holds a Moggleapp tablet, using it to continuously check his vital signs. Her attention is diverted by the shouting of two men who are engaged in a heated argument. The redheaded man walks over and snatches the woman's tablet. He looks familiar but in the low light it is difficult to make out just exactly who he is.

'Nurse Ming! We are down to our last two test cases, this project has been a complete disaster. VonHelmann won't be best pleased'! He berates her.

'Sorry Doctor, we did not anticipate the mutations being so tricky. They don't behave like humans, have many abnormalities'.

A second memory comes through of him playing in a small white room with another child, most likely around nine years old.

The boy looks familiar, with the same grey eyes. They throw a ball to one another, but he misses the last throw. Giving chase, the ball stops at the feet of a distressed-looking man, it looks a lot like Mad Newton. With a smile he picks up the ball and hands it to him, his palms though are sweaty and face very pale.

He tells him in a calm but firm tone, 'Dear, so very young, Van der Westhuizen. I have encoded memories of thy origins, to be reached at thy age of adulthood. I must use this needle to mask thy mind, or thy life will be endangered. Listen here... the Council must never know thy gift. Thy gift being even stronger than your source'!

He continues, 'Recall these memories, thy source, Martian President Van der Westhuizen, the Council expunged thee from history and his species. Thy genes are special, with it they seek to create an Elite force, capable of foreseeing events and dangers. Van der Westhuizen was no normal man, his gift though unrefined, some say it a mutation, others a disease. Trust me, it is a gift'.

Mad Newton pulls out a tablet and commences an interface. There is a 2D video of a man that looks remarkably like his present self, although a little chubbier, the same greyish blonde hair and grey eyes. Dressed in a tight-fitting white uniform, this man sits at a desk with a small flag, on it a red planet that must be Mars surrounded by its two moons, Phobos and Deimos. On his wrist, there are three numbers, *777*.

The interface continues, switching to an image of what appears to be a settlement, tagged *Mars One, Cydonia*. This settlement is made up of dozens of spherical pods bolted together, tightly packed into a rectangular shape.

Remembering his Universal Council's Wiki, he reads - *this place was the brainchild of a Dutch Entrepreneur, who helped to bankroll and organise the building of Mars's first privately funded manned outpost in Cydonia at the end of the 21st century, and was used for scientific research.*

This is where it starts to differ from the Wiki. The tag shows a much larger settlement with thousands of people; not a desolate sandy wasteland with few inhabitants, but green and prosperous like the Florida of 1998, with an area full of pod-like homes. He starts to remember what Mad Newton told him that the leaders on Earth at the end of the 25th century, then the Grand Council, decided that this planet was no longer insignificant. Seeing it now as a much-needed staging point and strategic base for its Spaceships and mining operations. The planet has many useful resources and technologies to exploit.

The Grand Council had initially planned to take it by force alone, however, the Martian's defensive technology was too advanced to penetrate. Mad Newton, his actual name Dr VonHelmann, thought he had won the argument to seek peace and bargain for Mars's green technology, putting the case forward that it could revitalise Earth. Unbeknownst to him, a group of high-ranking Elites led by Dr King had no interest in peace and its green technology. Dr VonHelmann was naïve to not realise that Earth's ill health played to their advantage and that they wanted to keep it this way.

They had hatched a most deceitful plot using Dr VonHelmann, then a junior interplanetary official, to broker an 'alliance' with the Martians including the signing of an agreement that would allow Mars to join the Grand Council and thereby creating the Universal Council. The Martians only saw honesty and warmness in Dr VonHelmann and could not foresee any deceit, just as he could not.

This Grand Council did not share power though. The agreement invalidated longstanding space neutrality laws and gave 'Universal' precedence to sanction the building of a grand armada, called the Space Army. Van der Westhuizen was completely caught off guard, his psychic ability unrefined and raw, he never looked further than Dr VonHelmann. More than that, his personal mantra to believe the best in others, even non-Martians, suppressed any misgiving.

Only after signing this agreement did President Van der Westhuizen foresee Mars's impending destruction, alas now too late to stop it. Having given them the ability to pass through Mars's defences with their newly formed armada, the Space Army, the

Martians could only wait for their impending doom. President Van der Westhuizen's body was taken by the Council to be studied. For the, now Universal, Council wanted to understand his genetics and purported Martian psychic ability, to harness its advantages for its forces. However, it is understood that after some time, research was put on hold and his brain cryogenically frozen. Too many tests had proven unsuccessful.

The mid-millennia marked a watershed in Earth's history. Ending a bloody and unstable period where many rebellions were quelled and the Council's leadership was finally won by Dr King. VanWest remembers more, Mad Newton told him the real story of the rise of the Council and Dr King, it started with a powerful core of Oligarchs that exploited Antarctica's refugees. Without a care for its human cost, many of these refugees were forced to work in mining operations, condemning them to a slow and painful death.

Dr King had started as an advisor to the Oligarch Bramsovica and over time his stature, as did his influence, grew. Together they purged their rivals in the Grand Council; accusing many of treason and other crimes, they sent most to penal colonies throughout the Solar System, never to be seen and heard of again. After that, Bramsovica went on to take a more discrete role, working behind the scenes as Dr King assumed the leading public-facing role as still seen nowadays in the Universal Red and Blue Games and Judgement Day.

Over the next 500 years, they promoted their own key people into important positions, including Commissioner Ming to Head of the Police Forces, Colonel Mason, his one-time Elite guard, to Head Enforcer in ColaBeers, and Four-star General Vladimir to Head of the Space Army. More recently, the promotion of Master Jiang to lead professor at the Enforcer's academy - only a century before was he an Elite guard to Dr King.

VanWest remembers Mad Newton's final words, his face still pale and hands sweaty, 'I am so deeply sorry for what happened to thy kind, the Martians. It plays on my conscience every day. For you, of Van der Westhuizen's genes, are more gifted than the Council knows. One day they will realise your gift but remember all

I have shown. Resist them! And help me return Earth to its Utopian self, the start of a New Beginning'.

With the interface ending, VanWest finds himself staring at his reflection in the mirror. Blood trickles down from his nose and his head pounds heavily, struggling to comprehend the deluge of memories that have flooded back. The truth of his and the Council's dark origins are overwhelming. For the first time he clearly sees the Council for what it is, the Elites abuse of power and their virtual enslavement of the citizens. Their rule more styled on the Roman empire than he realised, not just copied for the benefit of majestic events like that of the Universal Red and Blue Games. They too had a Council and enslaved many innocent people during their quest for ultimate power and the building of their huge empire.

'I am a Martian'! He struggles to grasp it as he says it out loud, more so that he is a genetically engineered replica of its last President. Disgusted with himself that he has been working for the murderer of his clone source and species, the Martians.

VanWest also struggles to understand why Dr VonHelmann, stayed with this evil Council for so long, centuries more in fact. It seems he used his last decades with them to figure out time-travel; inventing the Quantum Accelerator rod; and hiding his own secret mission to return Earth to its late 20th-century self. This 'New Beginning', an indication that he saw it easier to change the past than to fix the present, that it is beyond repair. He asks himself, is the Utopian's mission and actions in the past indeed so radical after all?

As he steps away from the mirror, he accidentally treads on the television's remote control, switching on to a channel '*CNN 6 o'clock News*'. There's a familiar image that of the astronauts tagged in the Priest's photos there's something very unexpected being reported. The Endeavour space shuttle, flight STS-88, is scheduled to launch today, Thursday the 3rd, close to 11pm!? The last photo tagged and list showed the 4th. This is a day earlier!?

Alarmed, VanWest checks his Wiki file once again to confirm the launch date. Finding that an attempt was actually made a day earlier, this means the astronauts will already be at the Launchpad, preparing. Reading the details on what happened, the launch of Endeavour was called off on the 3rd after the master alarm had been set off with no time left to restart the countdown and launch.

This was the first opportunity, in a small launch window of just a few days, for the launch of the Unity node to coincide with the passing of Zarya, the Russian built segment of the ISS. If the six astronauts are at Space Kennedy's Launchpad 39A, then Iris is likely going there too. Furthermore, with the Seductress still on the loose, she is in danger. Likely lurking close behind, looking to retrieve the Quantum Accelerator rod from her.

He foresaw this all in his vision at the end of Stage 3 of the Universal Red and Blue Games, the frizzy-haired woman and the wreck with the charred metal panel, *ENDEA*. This meant Endeavour. So very obvious now in hindsight. His mind returns to the likely scenario he thought of earlier, a popular NEA-Utopian tactic of blowing stuff up to kill all those inside. He must find Iris and convince her to find another way, convince her that they can build a bright future together, one built on trust and love.

Chapter 17   The Failed Launch

A sharp noise rings in his ears, a scrambled transmission coming through his Quantum Communicator, 'Captain VanWest! Report status! Come in... VanWest! Report status... come in'!

The memories and revelations about the Universal Council have opened his eyes. And whilst he has not yet chosen to side with the Utopians, he most certainly is no longer on theirs. He also knows the risk of answering, so manipulative and dirty are their tricks, their latest trying to influence his mind into killing Iris. It is time to start making his own decisions, his first priority finding his sweet Iris and protecting her from the Seductress.

'Captain... be sure to report status... come in... ' transmits through again from the Commissioner. Only, the transmission is even weaker and patchier than the previous one.

VanWest deactivates his Quantum Communicator. The Council no longer has power over him, certainly not in this past, for they no longer have a working Quantum Accelerator rod. However, the transmission does serve a useful purpose, confirming that the time continuum remains unaltered. The Council still being in control in the year 3000.

In order to infiltrate the Kennedy Space grounds and make it to Launchpad 39A, he will once again need a disguise. As shown on *CNN*, the astronauts are already in quarantine awaiting the first scheduled launch. Grabbing the box of *Popping Tarts*, he hurries from the apartment. Relieved to find his red Nissan rental car still parked, and the backpack of Ankit Bhargav 'the Priest' on the passenger seat. After figuring how to turn the funny knob on the car radio, he checks the various channels for news reports.

There are more channels than in 1951 Paris. By 1998 both FM and AM frequencies are available and is glad to find that there are 'no incidents' being reported on any. Taking out the facial remodulation kit, he rummages around to retrieve the NASA identity card, changing once again to this *Engineer D. Drake*.

With all that he has learnt, this notion of a 'New Beginning' still doesn't sit well. Changing the time continuum feels immoral and wrong. Furthermore, he's not convinced that Dr VonHelmann's Utopian mission will have the desired outcome he hopes for. It is not clear if these events in the 20th century are actually to blame for the rise of the Universal Council or a dystopian world in the year 3000. It seems the issue is more mankind's nature, not machine's, and its manipulation as Hans Ashtar philosophised. The Seductress a prime example of those working for their own selfish gains. Stopping this launch will only slow what comes after, be it a hundred or a thousand years delayed.

Using his Moggle X once again, he speeds out of *Horizon Drive* to head to the *NASA Causeway*, the fastest time to destination indicates *04:40:00* to reach Launchpad 39A. There's not much room for error, it's only five hours from the scheduled launch of Endeavour and its Unity node. Making matters worse, the traffic is laden with space enthusiasts and tourists coming to watch. With the sun setting, it's also getting much darker and harder to see.

It takes 25 minutes of swerving in and out of traffic down *Vectorspace Boulevard* to even reach the *NASA Causeway* and then longer to reach a drawbridge over the *Indian River Lagoon*, from where he hopes to reach Merritt Island, the home of Space Kennedy.

Watching his Moggle X's timer count down, taking a long-time to eventually reach this island. Chowing down the *Popping Tarts* as he drives, he needs the energy to stay alert. The taste is quite intriguing; oddly crusty on the outside with a fruity and sweet filling. Since arriving in this time, his diet has been high on sugar, a big change from his strict high protein diet as an Enforcer. It doesn't feel all that good, after an immediate sugar rush, it follows by giving him a slight migraine and stomach-ache. He can't quite believe that people actually ate this.

In the distance, with the help of his Moggle X, he sees a tall rectangular building in the dark. The Vehicle Assembly Building. It partly obscures an even more impressively tall building behind, and his target destination, Launchpad 39A. He zooms in to confirm it holds the space shuttle he's looking for; the long white spacecraft has a black nose tip with *Endeavour* written further across. Closer to its base, the *United States* is written alongside the NASA meatball logo in red, white and blue. It's the shuttle.

The emblem reminds him of his walk with Colonel Cornelius to Dr King's *Elite Quarters* on the SCC-400. Little did he know then that this meeting would end up with him being here, in 1998 Florida, at the home of NASA. So much has happened since.

The Launchpad is still estimated to be a long - *02:45:00* - time away, having taken him close to two hours to just to get just this far. A bottleneck ahead forces him to slow, where he spots a NASA security checkpoint, it is screening the vehicles that are coming to watch the launch, at the *Space Kennedy Visitor Complex*. Following the other drivers, VanWest winds down his window, hoping his disguise does the trick as he holds out the identity card of *NASA Engineer D. Drake*.

The security guard looks quite surprised, 'Sir! You work for NASA'!?

'Yep... Been called out for an emergency to Launchpad 39A'! VanWest reacts, improvising an excuse.

'Oh my! Better I get you fast-tracked'.

The guard immediately radios that he needs to make an urgent escort, signalling to VanWest to follow his vehicle as he turns his blue lights on, to head to the Launchpad. An unexpected piece of luck, the cars promptly moving out of their way. The estimated time to destination on his Moggle X drastically decreases as he drives behind, passing the Launch Control Centre and the Vehicle Assembly Building much faster than previously estimated.

Having saved him close to an hour and a half, the guard accompanies him right up to the perimeter's security gate. But he is still quite a distance from the Launchpad. The guard leaves, exchanging with him a salute before returning back to his checkpoint. The launch site is very flat, one big concrete slab with large patches of sand and in some places pools of water, swamps. There is barely anywhere to hide.

Getting to the Launchpad will require a new disguise, and despite saving so much time there's only *00:01:00* until the scheduled launch time, the countdown will already be underway. He doesn't want to risk using the NASA Engineers badge to go any further, the security is likely to get heavier. He recalibrates the facial remodulation kit to restore his own appearance but with one key addition - night camouflage: dark green stripes on darkened brown skin.

He pulls right and parks his car, opting to continue on foot. Leaving the flowery shirt inside, he proceeds semi-naked and bare-chested. Athletically hurdling over the first fence, he hurries and slips past a set of searchlights. It reminds him of his exercise courses at the academy on the Enforcer's moon base, except there he could at least find the occasional crater and rock for cover.

In front of the Launchpad is a shallow swamp. VanWest wades into the muddy water, doing his best to stay low and not make a splash. However, a searchlight suddenly falls on the lake, illuminating it across and forcing him to dive under the water. Holding his breath, he tries to stay calm, knowing time is of the essence.

The light soon moves on, half-crouched he exits. The swamp having given him an additional layer of camouflage, covering him in mud. Skilfully eluding a security patrol, he runs stealthily in the dark, a *00:20:00* run, until he reaches a low-level security fence that encircles the Launchpad. With another set of searchlights scouring the area around, he carefully navigates the razor-sharp barbed wire at its top, lifting himself up and over, where he lands inside the Launchpad's perimeter, the sand muffling his fall.

Straight ahead a dozen engineers wearing white lab coats inspect the launch rocket. Using his bionic sensors, he detects the signatures of the six-man crew inside the orbiter 195-feet above. Having already crossed the long swing arms, which connects the launch tower to the shuttle, they await lift-off in the white room of the Endeavour space shuttle. NASA very much aware of the poisonous gases emitted from the rockets; they stay in an environmentally hospitable room for protection. Unfortunately, this same awareness didn't lead to the creation of stricter international regulations, long before long-distance space travel took off with nuclear propulsion engines over the next two centuries.

An announcement staggers VanWest, T-minus 19 minutes, holding for another inspection'. His Moggle X now reads *00:19:00*; he believed he had more time.

Wondering if time is already beginning to shift, VanWest sets about surveying the area for Iris and the Seductress. His bionic sensors though return no matching signatures. But, as the engineers evacuate the blast area, he notices that one has not followed them. Instead, this engineer is walking towards, and not away from, the rockets!? Spotting an object in her hands, a primitive device called a walkie-talkie, he hones in to hear her speak.

'Houston, Florida, making one last inspection, over', the woman radios. Her voice isn't quite like that of Iris, but with the facial remodulation kit, she could have changed it along with her appearance.

'Standing by, awaiting your instruction', radios back Flight Control.

With all the other engineers out of sight, VanWest decides to intercept the woman. It's a gamble if it is not her he risks the alarm being raised and those watching in the Launch Control Centre.

The woman turns towards him as he approaches. It's indeed Iris, her electric blue eyes giving away her identity, having remained unaltered behind her thick-rimmed glasses. She holds in her other hand a tool, a silver circular Corrupter, not of this age. It also looks just like the one he foresaw during a moment of unconsciousness at the end of Stage 3 of Universal Red and Blue Games. He hopes the outcome will be different with no blast. Whilst the device is mainly used to corrupt electronic and mechanical systems, if left on maximum charge, it can detonate.

'Iris'! He calls out.

Iris takes a moment to realise that this striped man is him, 'VanWest? Is that you? ... My love, why did you come'?

'I can't let you kill yourself. I love you... I want us to build a new life. We have an opportunity to do so here', he pleads. Undeterred, she continues her sabotage, placing the Corrupter on the hydraulic pumps.

If it detonates, it could cause a chain reaction, blowing up the fuel tanks and all those in the immediate vicinity, the astronauts in the shuttle and herself. What's more, the whole explosion would look like a technical malfunction, the fault of the engineers.

'This is the only choice, my love... you MUST know that! The Council has destroyed everything. This is a sacrifice I MUST make', Iris explains, her voice breaking.

'My sweet. You can destroy the rod. It is the last working one. We can live here, together in the past. Help this world and time in other ways'.

'My love, it is not possible. Go, start a new life in this Utopia, you deserve it... ' Iris urges him. Reciting a line from one of Emily Dickinson's poem, 'Because I could not stop for Death - He kindly stopped for me'.

'T-Minus 10 minutes, evacuate the area'! Time seems to have speeded up.

As VanWest takes another step towards Iris, the sound of a gun cocking - *click* - stops him still. Their heads turn to find the Seductress dressed in a blue and black NASA security guard uniform pointing a black Desert Eagle gun at them.

'Hands up'! She strides over and takes the Quantum Accelerator rod from Iris's belt, knocking her Corrupter out of her hand as she does so.

'You two are pathetic. Dear Iris, I believe you are wanted for Judgment Day'! The Seductress taunts, as she activates the rod, which jolts out to create a black portal to a destination of her choice.

'I won't go alive'! Iris warns her defiantly.

'I see... well, I'll kill your lover if you don't go! You are both fools, your love repulses me, it disgusts me', the Seductress scolds as she gestures that she will shoot VanWest. Showing a hint of jealousy at VanWest's love for Iris and Iris's love for him.

Iris looks mournfully at VanWest, just like she did when leaving through the holoscreen in Ward B. He tries to think what he can do to stop the Seductress.

Before he can react, the Seductress shoves Iris inside and in a split second Iris disappears. Seeing Iris's Corrupter on the floor, he jumps towards it, narrowly dodging the Seductress's bullet - *pop* and grabs hold of it, ready to detonate. Locked in a stalemate, she thinks about aiming another bullet to disable it, but she needs a clean shot.

'Listen to me, VanWest. There's an opportunity for there to be no Judgment Day, one without Dr King, one without VonHelmann'! The Seductress tries to negotiate.

Waaahhhh! The sound of the gunshot has caused the alarms to sound. In the distance, he can see armed security guards racing towards them.

'This daughter of Mad Newton, I sent back to where she came. You can now think for yourself! Make your own decisions... Neither Dr King nor Iris's father care for us. Mad Newton wants the past for himself like King wants the present. Let us together shape a new world and time', the Seductress offers.

The portal's pull weakens and its whistling decreases, it is starting to shut. VanWest is unconvinced. He doesn't trust her, having already fallen for her tricks twice, in 1951 France and the Utopian's bunker. All he knows for certain is that he must rescue his sweet Iris, therefore stopping this Seductress and leaping back to the present. He slowly lifts his Electroskeleton hand, the Corrupter in his other hand.

He scowls, 'The past is neither yours nor mine to meddle with. My time is the present with Iris'!

The Seductress reacts by firing her gun - *pop* - destroying the Corrupter, careful to hit it so it doesn't explode. But before she can fire again, VanWest reacts with his Electroskeleton hand, sending out a powerful pulse - *whoosh* - that smacks into her and pulverises her entire body.

With the portal now closing, VanWest jumps back to his feet and leaps into it. Disappearing as the NASA's security guards arrive, confused to find that no one is there.

Chapter 18   Leap to Judgment Day

VanWest spirals through the portal and slams into the ground, sending a cloud of dust into the air. He rolls to his side, badly winded and struggling to breathe, his skin stinging and his head spinning. Flashes of Iris on her knees with a laser dagger against her slender neck cross his mind as a loud chant with his name rises, 'VanWest, VanWest, VanWest'!

Even though he still wears the baggy shorts of the Homestead pilot and his electroskeleton hand, his body no longer bears camouflage stripes. Mustering all his strength and balance, he presses his palms against the sand to clamber to his feet. As he foresaw, he is in a Romanesque gladiatorial arena lined with giant marble pillars. The chanting comes from stands filled with spectators in grey jumpsuits. Many are there in the flesh and not as holograms; a rare occurrence for only the most high profile of executions. VanWest realises that he has leapt to the Seductress's destination, Judgment Day! The day of executions!

The large holoscreens display his image in 4D. He looks nervously around and, as expected, finds Iris. Having been forced to her knees, she winces in pain as Alpha presses his laser dagger against her slender and once pale neck, now reddened and blackened from its searing heat. For all he could foresee, this 'gift' as both Dr VonHelmann and Dr King have called it, has done little to stop this from coming true. Seemingly it was inevitable that Iris would be here with him helplessly watching.

The silver Quantum Accelerator rod lies close to her partially buried and hidden in the sand. His visions intertwined with the

Seductress, she the one to transport them here, right to this spot, their fate.

As VanWest looks despairingly at Iris; unsure what to do, still slightly disorientated. A man shouts through the chants, 'Down with the Council'!

The voice sounds familiar. Looking to his right, he sees Dr VonHelmann, aka Mad Newton, his bruised body chained to a metal pole. He shouts again, 'Down with the Council'! He has been tortured, likely by the Interrogator, and given his final punishment, forced to bear witness to his daughter's execution at the hands of Captain Alpha.

Every Sunday, Judgment Day broadcasts live from the Colosseum. It is less an entertainment show than a propaganda tool for the Universal Council: an event used to terrify its citizens and deter those that may commit offences against them. Unsurprisingly, the Colosseum is linked directly to Queen Elizabeth's most notorious prison, aptly named *Lord Kitchener*, after a British Field Marshall who built the first concentration camps during the second Anglo-Boer war of 1900. This camp was used by the English army to force the Boers of South African to submit to its rule by starving their families, wives and children.

The mega-prison is laid out in three triangular sections; the pre-trial detention centre, the correctional facility, and the execution block. Most of those locked inside have only committed minor crimes, such as stealing food, medical supplies or are merely awaiting trial for no other reason than having been rounded up by the quadrotors.

In the Universal law system of guilty until proven innocent, just deemed to 'look' suspicious can get one arrested. Those in pre-trial undertake factory jobs such as making jumpsuits and shoes. They are the lucky ones. The others sent to work in the mines are never leaving. They are the property of the Oligarch Linus Sugar, the Mayor of Queen Elizabeth, and owner of this land.

Pre-trial doesn't apply to the NEA rebels and Utopians, deemed beyond rehabilitation. They bypass the detention centre and correctional facility altogether and are sent directly to the execution block to await Judgment Day. After endless tortuous dream sequences, simulating their execution over and over, the Council not content to kill them once, leave most praying for this day to finally arrive.

With the Seductress pulverised in 1998 Florida, the Universal Council has given VanWest this unwanted credit of bringing Iris to Judgment Day, hence the chanting of his name. She is to be executed alongside several fellow high-profile Utopians, making this Sunday a propaganda bonanza. Today's theme could as well be called *The Universal Always Wins*. These executions will be broadcasted across the Solar System to show the immense cost of defiance. Not only will Dr VonHelmann be executed, so will his own flesh and blood, his beloved daughter Iris, and his loyal followers.

Toom-ta-ta-toom! The trumpet sounds right on cue with Dr King's emergence in the gilded stand. Gigantic flags roll down on each side, one red and one blue. Like he foresaw, Dr King acts like an Emperor, dressed in the same ceremonial toga and golden leafed Corona as in the Universal Red and Blue Games.

Given the high-profile nature of the executions today, he is flanked by numerous high-ranking Elites, including Commissioner Ming, Oligarch Linus Sugar, and Colonel Cornelius. Other usually more reclusive Elites have also turned out to make it a real show of power. It's imperative to be seen at this execution, to make a powerful reassertion to its citizens of just who its superiors are.

Even the Oligarch Bramsovica, the elusive Mayor of ColaBeers, is there, standing in the back. His small head balancing on a long body with short legs, somehow reaching over 6 feet 8 inches high. VanWest is surprised to see Captain Kun-lee, standing behind Colonel Cornelius. No longer pale and lifeless, Kun-lee gives VanWest a discrete and honourable nod, an acknowledgement of when VanWest and Barys saved his life in Pytheas's Labyrinth. His task today is to guard the Elites, surveying the arena for any sign of trouble.

The citizens hush as Dr King's image replaces VanWest's on the holoscreen. He steps forward and unrolls an old paper scroll - the sacred writings of the Universal's commandments, written by the Wisemen of the Council. They are said to have saved mankind from doom. Though little is known about them beyond a short Universal Council approved Wiki entry. They are quite mysterious. Considered to be men of respect and repute, they are credited with stopping the chaos after the decline of Earth's superpowers by leading the citizens to a new and fruitful land, Antarctica.

'Citizens! Heed the laws by, which we live! Remember the three commandments! Lest I must say, the first to serve without question the Universal Council. The second to work for the progression of man and the Universal. And, the third, to destroy all those who defy the Universal Council'!

Toom-ta-ta-toom! The trumpet sound prompts the uni-browed and near Cyclops eyed Commissioner Ming to step forward and stand beside Dr King. The Commissioner waits for a few moments, posing with outstretched arms to build the suspense, before calling in a grave voice for the citizens to 'Recognise the crimes of the Utopians, the deviant and traitor Mad Newton and his daughter'.

Pointing demonstratively down at them, 'Today, on this here Judgment day, in this Colosseum, we exorcise the worst of the worst. Deviants called Utopians! Defiers of the sacred Universal commandments. Defiers of the Universal Council. They try to destroy our very existence, our progress, all for their own hedonistic gain. Be sure, today we show the might of the Universal'!

'Salve the Universal', the citizens chant in response.

Waiting several minutes, he hushes them with both hands, 'We thank the hero of the Universal Games, our Elite Enforcer VanWest! All Salve the Universal, and our hero'!

Prompting a new long chorus, 'Elite VanWest, all Salve thee, the Universal, all Salve thee'!

Dr King speaks next, 'Citizens! Lest we know, the only judgement that can be given today, on this sacred Judgment day, is one that befits their heinous crimes. The verdict can only be death... Death by fire and dagger'!

'Death, Death, Death'! The spectators chant in response whilst a drumroll begins - *da-da-dum*.

Dozens of blindfolded Utopians emerge, flanked by armed patrol androids. VanWest immediately recognises the cockroach farmer, from the Utopian's secret base. Now bloodied and bruised like the rest, he is forced to walk barefoot in a torn prison garb, his eyelids cruelly fused shut. The patrol androids lead them to the front of the gilded stand, where they are forced to kneel before Dr King and the Elites.

Da-dum-da-dum! The tempo of the drums increases as Commissioner Ming instructs the patrol androids to withdraw. A low-level forcefield encloses the prisoners, the first executions of this Judgment Day beginning.

The Universal Council known to make the whole spectacle as entertaining and gory as possible, a trapdoor opens within the forcefield, causing the spectators to fall silent. Commissioner Ming continuing to build the suspense, holding his arms out again for several seconds, the drums still pounding. Finally, he nods - *ROAR*, two large animals emerge, drawing much applause. These pretty but terrifying animals have two menacingly large front canines, the size of VanWest's arms, and paws the size of his torso.

Sabre-toothed cats! Judgment Day is known to occasionally feature long-extinct predators, cloned and brought back to existence, to give that extra wow factor. The Universal Council has outdone itself. The rapturous applause only serves to agitate these huge cats further, roaring louder and louder.

A frightened prisoner runs forward. But, even before he can reach the forcefield, one of the cats pounces. *Agh!* It shakes the man violently as if he were a mere rag doll, biting his head from his body and sending blood squirting across the faces of the other Utopians. Several of the prisoners start to howl in terror, further incensing the cats who turn on them next.

One ginger-haired Utopian begins to chant religiously, 'Trust in Utopia'! It is one of the *Most Wanted*, Cisco 'The Inquisitor', a senior preacher of Utopianism. Weirdly, he doesn't appear frightened, rather he looks content, his belief so strong he savours his soon to be martyr status.

Those still alive join the chant, 'Trust in Utopia', which enrages Dr King greatly.

Not waiting for the large cats to finish off their prey, he nods to move on to 'Death by fire'! Flames shoot out from underneath, engulfing their bodies, which turns their skin black and their eyes yellow.

Agh! The scene of their burning bodies is reminiscent of heretics being burnt at the stakes during the European Middle Ages. The horrific sight forces many in the stands to look away, while some even vomit. The Universal Council knows all too well that many watching empathise with these high-profile Utopians. This message is designed for them. Literally setting them on fire, in front of their very eyes, with-it burning their hopes for a more equitable and greener world.

VonHelmann shouts again, his voice hoarse, 'Down with the Council'.

Dr King lifts his clenched fist triumphantly towards the grey sky as the executioner's drum roll begins again - da-*dum-dum-dum* - this time more deliberately than before. A triumphant smile covers Dr King's face as the attention turns to Mad Newton and his daughter. Captain Alpha's laser dagger still pressed against Iris's neck. With this grand finale, the Universal Council hope it will spell the end of the Utopians, breaking their resolve and that of their sympathisers for good.

Alpha very much relishing the attention as it now turns to him, poses proudly as if he were an actual gladiator in a Roman Colosseum. He looks up at Dr King, waiting for his Emperor's signal to slice her throat, a thumbs down. Like VanWest, he too has received a great prize.

'Citizens! Our Enforcers and new Elites, VanWest and Alpha, captured these deviants. Lest we must say, their loyalty and skill pay homage to the might of the Universal Council and a warning to all those deviants that seek to destroy the progress of man and the Universal. Join me in celebrating the Elite VanWest and Elite Alpha!'

'Elite VanWest, Elite Alpha'! The citizens chant.

VanWest gazes at his beloved Iris, his mind swirling, what can he do to save her? Being an Elite doesn't taste sweet. In fact, it tastes bitter, disgusting. He knows he MUST act! The tempo of the drumroll - *da-dum-da-dum* - signals the commencement of her execution.

'Death by dagger'! Dr King starts a new chant, readying to give the thumbs down.

VanWest knows what he can and MUST do. This new title of 'Elite' gives him special privileges, including Universal broadcasting rights. He can now show everyone what he has seen, the cruelties. Broadcasting to Judgment Day's audience. He activates his Moggle X and interfaces with the network, instructing it to upload his memories tagged executions and massacres. Without obstruction, it intakes his memories and immediately updates the large holoscreens circling the arena.

It's live!

Gasp! The drumroll falls silent. His memories play in succession, images of the slaughtered elderly citizens near the power station in Queen Elizabeth, and the massacre of innocent civilians in the slums of ColaBeers after capturing the NEA leader. Even though many citizens would have heard rumours about these heinous and nefarious events, this visual eye witness account provides undeniable and gruesome evidence of what the Universal Council has done. All under the guise and justification of progression!

VanWest lifts his arms up and calls their attention, 'Citizens of Earth, citizens of the Solar System! You know me as the hero of the Universal Games, the hero that destroyed the Utopians. But citizens I am not a hero, I like you am the Universal Council's victim. We, victims of the Elites that murder innocents and plunder our worlds. Citizens, and fellow Enforcers, JOIN ME in arms! Rise up for your freedom! For your children and children's children! It must stop, it MUST stop today'!

A shocked Dr King overrides his upload and erases it from the network, but the damage has already been done. The chants have returned, now no longer for Utopians to be executed, 'Death to the Universal Council'!

VanWest senses the momentum and urges them on, 'Citizens and Enforcers, REBEL'!

Dr VonHelmann joins, calling on his followers, 'Utopians, fight! Fight till thy last breath'!

Their battle cry spurs the citizens into action as they begin to pelt Dr King's guards with their cockroach burgers and any other object they can find. Captain Kun-lee looks unsure how to react, as do the other Enforcers. Many have never witnessed such open dissent. Crucially, it is the Colonel's intervention that swings this scene in their favour, ordering them all to step back and not engage. It seems the Colonel harbours the same misgivings as VanWest.

A shocked Dr King shouts frantically to his new Elite, Alpha to finish the execution, finally giving the thumbs down. But VanWest, still armed with his Electroskeleton hand, reacts more swiftly and sends a shockwave - *whoosh* - that knocks Alpha back and destroys his dagger. The sight rallies the citizens further who race towards the Elite's gilded stand. With the Colonel not ordering the Enforcers to engage, only the patrol androids are left to defend the Elites.

An incensed Alpha sprints towards VanWest, tackling him to the floor before he can send another shockwave. His strength superior, he rips off VanWest's Electroskeleton hand, smashing it on the arena floor. VanWest counterpunches have little effect as Alpha's giant fists dig deep into his ribcage. With no body armour to protect VanWest, each fist bruises - *crack*.

Alpha's eyes narrow, now burning menacingly red, as he grabs VanWest by the throat and starts to choke him. His eyes like those of the Space Soldiers, his strength more machine than man. Worse, two metal blades jolt out from his wrists, thrusting one into VanWest's right thigh. Iris runs over to try and help him, but with her hands still bound, she is easily tossed aside with a knock of Alpha's elbow.

Next, the blades push towards VanWest's neck but, before they reach, flashes of orange light strike Alpha. His armour is not enough to protect him, and his skin is instantly incinerated. All that is left behind is a broken metallic skeleton, finally revealing his true self, a cyborg. It all makes sense now. The Universal Council has been experimenting with cyborgs as Enforcers.

Undeniable proof that the Council seeks to replace them, just as they replaced humans in the Space Army hundreds of years ago. The Colonel had hinted at this in the elevator after his interrogation and torture - the reason why the Colonel supports him now.

The light beam has also destroyed the silver Quantum Accelerator rod, in its place is a large hole. VanWest looks up to the gilded stand and finds, to his astonishment, that the Colonel is the one who fired the shot that saved his life. A mortified Kun-lee looks at Dr King and then at the Colonel, unsure what to do, as a still bound Iris runs into the arms of an injured VanWest.

One of the most influential Enforcers, a hero to most, has joined the uprising, and now shouts, 'The Enforcers of Queen Elizabeth are with VanWest'!

The citizens chant, 'Down with the Elites'! Further emboldened, they overwhelm the patrol androids guarding the

Elites; ripping their long limbs and weapons from their metallic bodies.

An enraged Dr King removes from under his toga a small diamond phaser and, in front of a confused and unsure Kun-lee, he fires a shot into the Colonel's back. The force so strong that it blasts his legs from underneath him and throws him out of the stand, onto the arena's floor.

The incensed citizens, having overwhelmed the bots, clamber into the gilded stand, sending Commissioner Ming and Dr King into retreat, shoving Mayor Linus Sugar into their path, buying them a few valuable seconds to transport to their ships stationed close by. The Mayor's screams - *agh* - echo across the Colosseum as he is mercilessly beaten and stamped to death.

Captain Kun-lee has, by default, become the most senior Enforcer left in the arena. Not knowing what to do, he orders a retreat. Both to avoid a confrontation with the citizens as well as to seek guidance from higher-ranked Enforcers: Colonel Mason of ColaBeers and Colonel Mathieu of Ellsworth.

VanWest limps over to a mortally wounded Colonel, 'Thank you'!

'Captain, it is I that thank you. Finally giving me the strength to defy the Council. Spluttering up gluts of blood, he continues, 'VanWest, your courage roaching inspired me... You showed everyone that the Council are not all-knowing, just a bunch of power-mad murderers'.

Coughing up more blood, he warns, 'Beware... their Space Army, they will amass over Mars and come to wreak revenge. Beware... your past... do not hesitate to... do not hesitate... to kill those evil doctors in their base'.

'Colonel, I don't understand. Which doctors? Which base'? VanWest replies.

The Colonel musters his final energy to lift his forearm, which ejects out a red diamond-shaped chip, 'MARS! Take this... the coordinates. Be-ware the doctors. And, most of all, BE-WAR-E YOURSELF', he shouts with his last dying breath.

Mars? Doctors? Myself? VanWest has so many questions to ask but the Colonel passes away. He thought the Council's main base was on the Moon, alongside the Enforcer Academy.

VanWest takes a brief moment to pay his respects, a small salute. Iris has to pull him away, 'We have to get out, your leg is bleeding badly'.

VanWest struggles to comprehend the Colonel's final words but he knows that he must go and find this base on Mars, using his chip for directions. Iris helps him towards her father, who is still chained against the metal pole.

The citizens now overrunning the arena's floor, continue to chant in defiance, 'Death to the Universal'!

Chapter 19   A New Beginning

Iris embraces her father, 'Papa! Papa! I love you'!
Dr VonHelmann replies, 'My love, so happy you have been saved. Praise be'.

A big brawny brute of a man with a black beard and moustache is barging through the citizens. VanWest, at first, believes him to be a danger and tries block his way but, to his astonishment, the burly man embraces Iris, lifting her up like a child.

'Pretoria! Am I glad to see you'! Iris welcomes him with a smile.

'Me too. We make quick now'! Pretoria breaks their restraints with his Corrupter device, Iris holding her father's much-weakened body upright.

They must leave the Colosseum as fast as possible. Not only because of the risk of large sabre-toothed cats attacking once the weakened forcefield fails, but also the SCC class ships of Dr King and Commissioner Ming that hover close by. They could strike down at them.

'Hey, help him first'! Iris calls on Pretoria to go to the aid of VanWest who struggles to walk with his injured leg.

Pretoria glares angrily at VanWest, to him this is no friend, 'Him'?!

'Yes, do what she asks'! Dr VonHelmann instructs.

Pretoria shakes his head sideways but agrees, reluctantly lifting VanWest's arm over his shoulder, as Iris helps her father. They head for the entrance of the arena to a giant metal door that has been opened. VanWest looks around, dismayed to see that all the Enforcers have left, hoping more would come from the Colonel's rally. With them gone, the Universal Council will not hesitate to eradicate all those left inside.

Working together to reach the entrance, the holoscreens suddenly go dark and a dissonant - *grumbling* - noise roars through, so strong it nearly knocks them off their feet. A long and narrow vessel uncloaks, a ship VanWest knows all too well, the SCC-400. The citizens stare stupefied up at it. A second ship follows, a slightly older version of the same class, the SCC-300, which belongs to Commissioner Ming. VanWest urges the group to continue to the entrance.

For the citizens, it takes a few valuable seconds to realise what is about to happen, and then to react. Screams of terror breakout as they flee, trampling over one another to find an escape. Some willing to even risk death by jumping over the arena's walls. Having moved faster, VanWest and the group are closer to the entrance but it could be too late for them too.

A white light jolts down from the SCC-400, causing Pretoria to throw VanWest against the wall before jumping on top of Iris and Dr VonHelmann to shield them with his large frame. Row by row, the citizens disappear. Narrowly stopping short of them by only a few yards. Not waiting for its return, they scramble through the metal door.

Waaahhhh! Sirens wail outside as patrol androids swarm the area. Still no clearer on what the Enforcers have decided to do; there is not one Enforcer in sight. Pretoria helps them to a nearby transport hub as the laser and proton shots from the patrol androids, now encircling the colosseum, whizz past, incinerating - *boom-boom, boom-boom* - everything they hit. Having heeded their call, the NEA rebels engage, several waiting in front of the hub, bravely returning cover-fire to allow them to make their escape.

Hurrying inside, a flash of light immediately transports them to another hub located in Downtown, Queen Elizabeth where

Pretoria rather unkindly throws VanWest down. Iris helps her father to lean against a wall for support. They take a moment to catch their breath.

The uprising is now in full effect. The streets overrun by citizens carrying makeshift weapons, some only armed with stones and knives to engage in pitched battles against Quadrotors and androids. Above, several NEA Battleships, spirally and pointy in design, target the bot operated security installations. VanWest's upload and rousing speech providing the fuel to ignite the citizens into action, now helped by the arriving rebels.

In the distance, smoke rises from the buildings on either side of the tall Enforcer HQ in Mid-City. Captain Kun-lee likely having already retreated there.

'VanWest, pardon me, I haven't completed an introduction, this is the head of the NEA in Queen Elizabeth'! Dr VonHelmann introduces Pretoria.

Very much angered by VanWest's involvement in the NEA leader's death in ColaBeers, Pretoria isn't so welcoming, 'This make no friendly greeting, you make my friend tortured in ColaBeers and then killed'.

Dr VonHelmann, keen to ease the tension, answers, 'Thank you for getting us out of the Colosseum, but I ask you not to blame VanWest. He only followed orders. Let us not lament but praise those sacrificed. Let us trust in Utopia and in this New Beginning it brings us'!

VanWest inserts the Colonel's chip, in one of his nodes behind his ear, adds, 'Pretoria, I did not understand their evil. Even what evil was. But I need your help to stop Dr King. The Enforcer Colonel, Cornelius, warned that the Space Army would amass in Mars, and gave me coordinates to a secret base... in Arcadia, near a volcano named Alba Mons. I can find him'.

A surprised Dr VonHelmann interjects, a hint of concern in his voice, 'Alba Mons? I know of it. There was a base there once... I thought it to be abandoned long ago'.

'Get me to Mars undetected, and I will kill Dr King', VanWest offers, looking at both Dr VonHelmann and Pretoria for their support.

'Doctor, me make not help this Enforcer. Me need ships in the air, fighting here'! Pretoria objects, pointing up to his Battleships now crisscrossing the skies. Moreover, he doesn't trust the words of an Enforcer, changed or not.

Dr VonHelmann pushes him to reconsider, his tired face more serious and frowned, 'Pretoria! VanWest can destroy the Council... Dr King. Trust in Utopia and thus him'!

Pretoria is one of a rare few NEA rebels to not heed Utopianism, at least not so doggedly. He looks unconvinced at the idea of working with VanWest.

'Yes, Pretoria. You MUST trust'! Iris appeals.

Her pleas seem to work better, their bond is closer, having worked together on the ground in Queen Elizabeth for many years, 'Ok Doctor, I can make trust. Contact in New Jersey help. Speak funny Warlord called Method A. Make to New Jersey first, then make to Mars second on cargo ship'.

'Thank you'! Dr VonHelmann replies.

'Make fast, they make unspeakable revenge on citizens if not'.

'Thank you'! Iris hugs Pretoria, 'Take good care of my father, ensure he gets medical attention, before anything else'.

Pretoria nods and then signals over a blackened out hovercar that waits across the street. Its gull-winged doors lift open, and a man with pointy ears peers out. Dr VonHelmann recognises him, as does VanWest, albeit for a different reason, for it is one of the Universal Council's *Most Wanted*, Charlie LeSouris 'the Hacker'. A small *U tattoo* under his right ear, indicating that he too is a Utopian. It seems not all the high-ranking Utopians have been killed after all.

'Praise be to Utopia! Is that you? You my favourite geek, you finally show thyself'! Dr VonHelmann greets his friend, but calls him out too for not being there for the leap to the 'New Beginning'.

He jokes, his voice though sad, 'Unlike some, I am too clever to walk into an Enforcer trap, you old fool'! Looking a little more sombre, 'My friend, they surrounded the bunker and blocked all communication channels. I could not hack my way through to send a message'.

'It was for the best you were not there'! Dr VonHelmann commiserates. They pause for a moment to think of all those lost in the last few days, including the martyring of Cisco 'The Inquisitor' and Lexi LuLu 'The High Priestess'.

'This was not in vain'! Dr VonHelmann adds.

VanWest knows he needs to tell them what happened, that these lives need not have perished, 'It was the Seductress who betrayed you. Dr King was tracking you for a long time. She told them of the bunker. She also murdered Ankit, your Utopian priest'.

Dr VonHelmann returns a look of disbelief, in 700 years has he rarely been betrayed by one so close, especially by a dedicated Utopian.

Iris explains further, 'Yes, father! She brought me back to Judgment day, not VanWest'!

Dr VonHelmann shakes his head, left speechless, with Pretoria the first to respond, now even keener to help, 'That make me sad... We must make trust in each other now. LeSouris make it to New Jersey, to Method A, warlord make help VanWest to Mars'.

LeSouris is keen to help too and knows Method A well, 'My friends, I agree. If Mars holds this New Beginning, I will help... This warlord and casino boss, we work together before, she have many cargo ships for smuggling'!

Dr VonHelmann nods and turns to Pretoria, 'Thank you for all you have done today. I will join you to lead the insurrection here, so we can muster a fleet to aid VanWest on Mars. There, we will finish the Space Army once and for all. Trust in Utopia'!

'I make yes! We sort out Queen Elizabeth first', Pretoria agrees, signalling a second waiting black hovercar to come over. Whilst he is not a staunch adherent to Utopianism, he is well respected and trusted. By a twist, if it were not for his lack of belief, he might have been at the Utopian bunker and not be here to support them now.

Dr VonHelmann takes Iris's hand, 'My love, I will take you to a safe house, we can then coordinate plans to organise an army from Earth's new resistance: the citizens, Utopians and NEA'.

An annoyed Iris pulls her hand away, 'Father, no... I'm going with VanWest'!

'But, my love, you cannot! I nearly lost you in the Colosseum, I can't bear to see you in harm's way again', Dr VonHelmann pleads, as a father does for his daughter, wanting to protect her.

'It's my choice'! Iris protests.

VanWest sides with Iris, he wants her by his side, 'Iris has my vote. She infiltrated Ward B successfully as Nurse Rose. Her infiltration skills will be invaluable'.

Dr VonHelmann's words have also triggered an idea that could help to bolster Earth's resistance army. Captain Kun-lee owes VanWest honour for saving his life. He thinks Dr VonHelmann can call on this, given Colonel Cornelius's call to the Enforcers of Queen Elizabeth to join as well. Requesting Kun-lee to facilitate ceasefire talks, maybe even a new alliance with the Enforcers.

'Yes! Exactly! Papa, I'm going, and that's final', a stubborn Iris tells him in a firm tone.

'Do not worry, she will be safe with me', VanWest reassures.

Dr VonHelmann is left with no option but to relent, replying in a firm tone of his own, 'VanWest, I will hold you to that'.

Giving one final fatherly advice to Iris, 'My love, if it must be, then it comes with one condition... on the first sign of trouble, you must run. Agreed'?

'Agreed'! Iris smiles, her fingers crossed behind her back.

It's time to go. As Iris goes to bid Pretoria farewell, Dr VonHelmann shuffles over to VanWest. Taking him to one side, he asks, 'By any chance, do you have still a Quantum Communicator'?

VanWest nods and hands it over to him.

'Very good'! Dr VonHelmann fiddles with the controls, resetting it so it cannot be tracked and then reprogramming, 'To contact us, enter the code 0-1-0-3-4-5-8-9-X, I repeat 0-1-0-3-4-5-8-9-X. This is our secret channel, if you send a message, only I and those I share it with will see it'.

VanWest makes his suggestion, 'Dr King made a massive error in killing Colonel Cornelius. This is my and the Enforcers' hero. They are in shock, now is the time for dialogue with them'.

Dr VonHelmann looks at him, intrigued to hear more. Moving slightly further away from Iris and Pretoria, he urges VanWest to reveal more, 'Go on'.

'Did you see the Enforcer, Captain Kun-lee? Standing beside the Colonel in the gilded stand'?

'I saw, yes', Dr VonHelmann replies.

'He owes me his life. There is honour between us. You know of the Enforcer code of honour'?

'Of course, yes'. VonHelmann has not only heard of the Enforcer's unbreakable code of honour but was also there at its creation.

'Call it in my name... Kun-lee is at the Enforcer HQ, ask him to grant you an audience with the higher-ranking Enforcers, Colonel Mason and Mathieu. The Enforcers will listen, they have seen Alpha, they have heard Colonel Cornelius's call. The Colonel knew, as do the other Colonels, that the Council seeks to replace the Enforcers with Space Soldiers'.

'VanWest, be assured that I will. This can be a New Beginning for the Enforcers as well. They will have an opportunity to become free Enforcers in Earth's new resistance army, may it be called E-a-R-A. Praise Utopia'! Dr VonHelmann answers with a big smile, excited at the prospect of Enforcers joining the resistance. VanWest hopes that Kun-lee will have enough courage to honour his request.

Dr VonHelmann, in a lower voice, warns him about this base he now leaves for, 'VanWest, these coordinates the Colonel gives. Thy origins are there. I worry to tell thee'.

VanWest heard the same warning from the Colonel, and also in a low voice replies, 'I played the chip you gave, I saw what happened to Van der Westhuizen. I saw a lab and the cribs. I remember it all. This is not from the moon, it is from this place, correct'?

Dr VonHelmann grabs his hand, trying to make it look as if they are wishing each other goodbye, 'You know now of the betrayal of thy people. I once saw Utopia on Mars... the Council only a threat. This ginger-haired man, their Head of Science, Doctor Minus Schuurman has another lab there, but I warn... Only wickedness resides inside'.

Squeezing his hand harder, he adds in a chilling voice, 'Kill them all'!

With encouragement from Iris, Pretoria reluctantly walks over to VanWest, extending his hand. Pretoria's mixed feelings still very much apparent as he squeezes tightly. He then goes to help Dr VonHelmann to the second waiting hovercar, who immediately tells him of VanWest's recommendation that they must seek out Captain Kun-lee to invoke the code of honour and try to persuade the Enforcers to join Earth's resistance army, EaRA.

The truth is stark, if the Space Army led by Four-star General Vladimir amasses then everyone's life will be in peril. The EaRA needs more allies to counter and fight them, whilst hoping that VanWest can find and kill its ultimate leader and mastermind, Dr King.

VanWest too contemplates Dr VonHelmann last words, 'Only wickedness resides there'. He is both fearful and curious as to what he will find.

Supported by Iris, he limps inside LeSouris's hovercar where he is welcomed by a silver pincher device. Before he can ask any questions the pincher jabs him several times, disabling any foreign object that could be used to track them. LeSouris has been named 'the Hacker' for a good reason; adroit at circumventing the Council and their security, he knows well how not to be found and he's not going to take any risks here.

As the door slams shut, the vehicle spins and accelerates rapidly towards the highway, moving swiftly through the black smog and away from any bots. In the skies above, more NEA Battleships have entered the fray, with deafening shot after deafening shot ringing out - *boom, boom.*

With the probing complete, Iris sets about healing VanWest's leg wound. With an old-tech medical kit, she smears a convalescing cream on the wound and wraps it an aluminium bandage. She also rubs some on his broken ribs. VanWest returns her help, rubbing some of the ointment over her wounded neck, instantly relieving the pain and redness.

Thanks to LeSouris's speedy driving they are soon inside the Warehouse District where he pulls into an inconspicuous storage unit. Its magnetic door opens to reveal a hangar about 30-feet tall, strangely though there is no ship inside, stacked instead full of black crates. VanWest gives Iris a confused look.

However, as LeSouris drives further inside, the crates start shifting, slowly transforming into a circular craft with a red eye on top. It was all just an illusion, a clever disguise. This ability to hide is one of the reasons the NEA and Utopians have been able to operate so effectively in the settlements.

The craft is very old, a throwback to the times of primitive transporters. Its build a stark contrast to what VanWest is used to, the ultra-modern and dynamic Enforcer patrol ships. Its frame is round and cumbersome, neither sleek nor dynamic. It has holes for windows, covered by black metal shutters and re-enforced glass, with no electric shield to protect itself. Furthermore, there is no transporter beam to enter inside. Instead, they must use a pull-down hatch. The gulf in technology between this craft and an Enforcer patrol ship so very large.

LeSouris presents it proudly, cracking a light-hearted joke as he does, 'VanWest, I introduce you my oldest friend, well other than Iris's father! He is Hawkeye... Do not judge by appearance, he is like me, he is more spritely than any half his age'!

'Ah, the handsome Hawkeye. So glad to make your acquaintance again'! Iris answers with a smile, having been on this craft before.

'How old is this rust bucket? It must be four hundred, five hundred years old... Is it even safe to fly'? A flabbergasted VanWest inquires, causing Iris to grin. Quite concerned as to how it will get them to New Jersey as Pretoria instructed.

'My friend, in fact, yes! His age, you may perceive weakness, but no, no, it is great strength! You see, he has prototype cloaking technology and engine, undetectable to Universal sensors. It can fly undetected', LeSouris explains.

'It is green tech, it charges by sunlight', Iris explains more plainly.

Hawkeye's green technology makes it a real Utopian favourite. Unlike many crafts before and after, it does not emit radioactive gamma particles. By using green technology, it can circumvent the Council's sensors, more tuned to pick up spikes in radioactive particles, allowing LeSouris to move between settlements without being spotted.

'Ok, wonderful! Another question, will we suffocate to death before we get to New Jersey'? VanWest asks sarcastically, the cockpit so very small.

'Shut up! And take a seat'! A still grinning Iris nudges him.

They pull down the hatch and squeeze inside one by one. LeSouris hands a grateful VanWest a white jumpsuit along with some all-terrain boots from the rack. Having arrived semi-naked from 1998 Florida, his chest has reddened from the high heat levels and radiation prevalent in Queen Elizabeth.

'Ah, you look civilised now'! LeSouris jokes.

Iris and VanWest take a much-needed moment to relax on their chairs. Not only have they travelled through time, but they have also dodged death a number of times both in the past and the present. LeSouris hands them both some capsules, full of vitamins and proteins. For VanWest, a welcome change from the high sugar diet of 1998 Florida. At least this doesn't give him a stomach-ache.

Trying to be helpful, VanWest offers, 'By the way, I still have my Moggle X. It will notify me of any approaching Enforcer ships'.

LeSouris gasps, 'No! I thought my pincher take it. Switch off immediately. No electronic devices, Universal monitor pick it up'.

VanWest nods, somewhat embarrassed, 'Not a problem'.

'Ok, lady and gentleman sit back and enjoy the ride. We'll be in New Jersey in no time', LeSouris activates stealth mode and starts the engine.

Hawkeye shakes violently as it readies to launch, the storage unit's roof opening, VanWest copies Iris and LeSouris, who hold onto their seats. The craft powers up and thrusts up into the sky.

VanWest takes Iris's hand as the stealth craft stabilises. Peering through the shutters, they are shocked to see the capital, Queen Elizabeth, in ruin. Many of its transportation hubs and skyscrapers having been flattened and reduced to smouldering rubble. Even the once green and iconic Vitali Sun Terra, a symbol of the capital's opulence and greatness, burns. This 'New Beginning' in full flow, its success, a new age for Antarctica and Earth, now rests at least partially on their shoulders.

Read More

VanWest
The Present

FIRST EDITION
KDP ISBN: 979-8-64723036-2

Out July/August 2020
Book 2 in VanWest Series

Follow on Facebook and Twitter @VanWestbooks

VanWest The Past - British English language edition.
We would love to have your feedback on Amazon or Goodreads.

Printed by Amazon Italia Logistica S.r.l.
Torrazza Piemonte (TO), Italy